Chocolate Cake and a Corpse

Murder in Moorbank: Book One

SUSI J. SMITH

DEDICATION

This book is dedicated to all the people who want the
simple things in life, such as being paid to dream.

ACKNOWLEDGMENTS

I'd like to thank:

West Lothian Writers for all their help and support over the years(and for not throwing me out)

Cheryl Baker for my fantastic book cover (I never realised how picky I was until we started)

My beautiful Bug, for letting Mummy write. Blackmail may or may not have been involved (just don't tell your dad)

Moffat, for trying (and repeatedly failing) to control our child. Pest. And for helping me find the time to write

And Derek Fleming, for sharing your knowledge of occupational therapy and how it has changed over the years.

CHAPTER ONE

"You've never worked, Mrs McIntyre." The recruitment consultant glares at my CV. Her comment elicits giggles from my fellow jobseekers.

The premises of Moorbank Recruitment Consultancy — a big name for a small town — are surprisingly spacious. A row of offices lie to my left, we could have met in there, but that would have been far less humiliating. Instead, I sit on a hard wooden chair, while the rest of the unemployed are lined up on seats behind me.

"It's Nora, and you're right, Karen—"

"Miss Brown."

Not the friendly-type then. This isn't going as well as I'd hoped. Last night I convinced myself I'd walk out of here with my dream job. Right now, I'd settle for leaving with my head still attached.

"I trained as an Occupational Therapist—"

"Twenty-five years ago."

"Twenty-four years ago." Can't she do simple subtraction?

Miss Brown's eyes narrow and I hurry on. "But that's when I started the course. I finished twenty-one years ago."

"And never bothered to practice." She throws my CV onto her desk. "All that time in higher education must have been *very* rewarding. What was it? A ploy to get Daddy to pay more attention?"

More giggling. Two redheads sit huddled together, chuckling and glancing in my direction. Thankfully the rest of the queue is not paying attention, or at least, they're pretending not to. A man in a white t-shirt scrolls his mobile, while a plump woman stares down at the book in her hand.

The redheads snigger again.

My cheeks flush. "Well—"

"So your licence lapsed."

"Yes."

"Nineteen years ago."

Oh, so that maths she can do. Is she like this with everyone? If so, it's a wonder any jobs get filled in this town. It can't be personal, I doubt she was even born when I left Moorbank.

A worrying thought comes to mind. Unless it's not about me.

I returned to Moorbank three months ago and had barely stepped off the bus when a woman started shouting insults at me. I thought she might be the local lunatic until Mum arrived in her yellow three-door Mini and it became clear that the two knew each other. Or rather, it became clear that Mum knew the irate woman's husband… intimately.

Was it possible Mum had done something to upset Karen too? I decide against asking.

"I'm hoping to retrain. I've already—"

"So…" Karen leans back in her chair. "You have no experience, no references, and no skills. It's amazing employers aren't beating down your door."

"I have skills." I wish I sounded surer.

"Sending your husband off to work with a peck on the cheek is not a skill." She raises her voice, no doubt hoping to produce more laughter from her friends in the audience. It works.

I clasp my hands together to hide the trembling "I can cook."

"Did you go to catering college? Or was it finishing school?"

"Well, no… And I'm not that posh, or rich."

Karen glances at the Louis Vuitton handbag resting on my lap, her meaning clear. I open my mouth to point out that the bag, a fortieth birthday present from my husband, is hardly the latest season's, when I catch myself. That wouldn't help.

"What about waitressing?"

"Do you have silver service training?"

"Do I need it? I could work in a café, surely they don't demand such things." Certainly not around here.

She smirks, flicking back her blonde hair. "Other candidates, young candidates, come in here with all the qualifications they need."

I bite my cheek, I can't afford to lose my temper, not now. "I'm forty-two, it's hardly old."

Karen looks horrified, I'm not sure she knew numbers went that high. In her eyes, I'm practically mummified. But my hair is still brown. It may not be natural, or even a high-end salon job — not anymore — but it's brown. And my figure's still reasonable. I'm a size twelve, at five foot five that's not bad.

I pull myself together. "I could clean."

"You'd have to do it yourself, Mrs McIntyre, not send a servant."

I could slap you. By myself. I'm sure of that. "I *can* clean," I say the words firmly, purposefully.

"Would you be willing to enrol in Moorbank Community College and gain a National Certificate in Cleaning? At your own expense, of course."

"Is there such a thing?"

Karen scoffs. "Obviously. It'll only cost you…" She

taps away at her computer keyboard. "Five hundred pounds. Bargain, to be qualified to clean the office toilet."

I sigh. "I could babysit, what qualifications do I need for that? Or is being a sixteen-year-old girl a mandatory requirement that I don't meet?"

"There's no need to be rude, Mrs McIntyre."

I disagree but manage to stop myself from saying so. "Sorry." The word escapes through clenched teeth. "What would babysitting require?"

Karen rolls her eyes dramatically and then marks off her answer on her fingers. "First Aid Training, an HND in Childhood Development, a National Certificate in Food Hygiene, I could go on."

My shoulders slump. "I need a job, Kar—, Miss Brown. I'll do anything, I don't care what."

"I think we have different definitions of 'need', Mrs McIntyre. Mine doesn't involve designer handbags and luxury cruises. Well, it does. Sadly, some of us have no choice but to work."

Ah, that may explain her attitude towards me. I almost feel bad for thinking Mum had something to do with it. Almost.

Karen leans forward, pointing to the people patiently waiting. "See that fat woman there, with the book. She gets her clothes from the donation bin at Alderlay's. And the redhead with the ankle tattoo, I've seen her going into a charity shop in Moorbank, and not to donate."

The group look annoyed by Karen's comments, but nobody is brave enough to challenge her and she continues. "They're not here to give themselves an amusing quirk to talk about over champagne cocktails. Go home, ask hubby to up the allowance, and let me help someone who needs it."

She sorts through the papers on her desk, a smile fixed on her face. I wish I could slap her and storm out.

My lip trembles. "My husband's dead."

Karen's ignorant smile falters.

My voice cracks. "I'm bankrupt. And homeless." My polished Edinburgh accent slips as I rise to my feet, leaning over her. "Yes, my bag is designer, but it also happens to be one of the few possessions the sheriff officers let me keep before throwing me onto the street and driving off in my car. Believe me, I understand 'need', and as I say, I need a job. Your job is to find me one, not to judge me."

There's a smattering of applause from my fellow jobseekers. They're my audience now.

Karen sighs, defeated. Digging through a folder, she hands me a crumpled sheet of paper.

"Hall-In Care is looking for carers. Ideally, they'd want someone with experience but not many people are *that* desperate for work."

"It's perfect. How do I contact them?"

"Well, if you'd bother to read what I just gave you, you'll see the number's on the bottom."

I peer at the job description, subtly moving it further away. One day I'm going to have to stop being so vain and buy some reading glasses.

"It's minimum wage so you might want to…" She indicates my clothes. "Supermarket chic is more in-keeping. They'll give you a tunic but you'll need to provide your own trousers and shoes."

I nod. "Thanks, I'll phone them now."

"They'll be delighted, I'm sure." Karen sneers and turns to her computer, dismissing me.

I head back to Mum's Mini, my fingers fumbling with the keys. With any luck, I could have a job by the end of the week. And better yet, a job that will let me brush up on my occupational therapy skills.

Exiting the car park, I drive through the town. To my right, hidden in a housing estate, lies the library. I used to be a regular, heading there straight from school, raiding the shelves for new books, and feasting from the community café. Then I'd trudge home in time for bed. Mum usually rolled in sometime later, her heels slipping as she stumbled up the steps, shushing her latest companion as they fell through the door in search of a bed.

From what the mad woman at the bus station was saying... yelling... it doesn't sound like much has changed.

CHAPTER TWO

"What a jumped-up wee madam, you should have kicked her. Accidentally, of course." Mum hands me a mug. "Who does she think she is, treating you like that? Your great-great-grandfather was the vicar here, back in the day. Did you tell her that?"

"Funnily enough, it didn't come up." I pull out a chair and sit down at Mum's teak kitchen table.

"You should have made it, turn the conversation to your advantage." Smoothing out a bump in the bohemian rug, she sits opposite me.

Her kitchen is chaotic, with stacks of papers mingling with tins of food and cutlery on the work surfaces. When I first moved back, I made the mistake of putting things away. Mum was furious. Apparently, there's a system I don't know about.

I sip the tea before subtly spitting it back into the mug and eyeing the greasy residue on top. How does she manage to make it so unpalatable?

Mum pops open a tin of biscuits. "So, when do you start?"

"I have to interview first." Something I haven't done since I was eighteen.

"They're lucky you're giving them the time of day." She stabs her tea with an already soggy biscuit.

"Karen implied otherwise."

"But you've got one? An interview?"

I nod. "They said they'd squeeze me in tomorrow." By the sounds of things, Karen was wrong about people not being, as she put it, 'that desperate for work'.

"You should have told them who you really were."

She says that like I use an alias.

Mum gestures with her biscuit. "We Jameses have a name in this town."

A reputation more like.

"Granddad robbed the bank, it's hardly something to be proud of." Although, I know she is.

Mum straightens up. "I turned out all right."

I attempt to spoon the grease from my cup. "Except for having me out of wedlock." In a small town like Moorbank, that's still a big deal now, let alone back then.

"How long did they call you Unmarried Marian?"

She sniffs. "It was Maiden Marian. And they still do." Suppressing a grin, she continues. "So what does this job involve anyway?"

"Care in the community. Helping the elderly to stay independent."

"Wiping bums more like." She slurps her tea. "What's the pay?"

"Minimum wage." Whatever that is. "But it's regular work and a step towards getting back on my feet."

"Minimum wage? Given house prices round here, you'll have the deposit for a one-bed flat by…" She stares at the ceiling, mouthing the maths. "The time you die."

She has a point, I'll be lucky to clear the debts Colin left before I'm due to retire.

I toss the teaspoon onto the table. "I don't seem to be qualified for anything else. And even if I was, Karen Brown's not going to help me get it. Not unless I bribe her with my handbag."

"So why don't you?" Mum licks her finger then uses it to gather up the remaining biscuit crumbs. "How many of those fancy-dancy clothes of yours do you think it'd take?"

"I'm not bribing her."

She shrugs. "Has she got a boss? Maybe you could speak nicely to him. You know, in a tight blouse. I could lend you one if you like."

I can only imagine what she has in mind. Leopard print perhaps, with a plunging neckline. "Maybe next time."

She looks ridiculously pleased with my response. Mum and I have very different ideas about fashion. I prefer things simple and classy. Mum is a bit... louder. Today's ensemble is a canary yellow velour tracksuit, with a low-cut luminous pink top underneath. With her cherry hair, she's hard to miss.

"You off out tonight?" I ask, more to change the subject than out of any genuine interest.

"Naturally. This is my second date tracksuit." She strokes a sleeve.

"The woman at the bus station, is this..." I indicate her clothes. I don't really want to know, but suppose I'd best be prepared for further verbal assaults.

"Course not, he's dead. Anyway, I don't sleep with married men."

That's not what his wife thinks. "I'm sorry. When did he... pass?"

She scoffs. "Dead's dead, Nora. And it was ten years ago. Old Aggie just likes the sympathy. As if I'd look twice at her Ben." Mum straightens up, inadvertently sticking out her ample chest. She may not have looked twice at Ben, but I'm certain he noticed her.

"Why don't you come tonight? It'd do you good to get out." She looks me over, frowning. "You know, Mikey has a friend, Robert. Bit handsy, but he's got a great sense of humour if you don't mind a bit of casual chauvinism."

I search for the right words, then give in. "I'd rather shave my eyelids with a potato peeler."

"All right Crabbit Annie, it's not my fault Colin—" She stops abruptly and rises to wash her cup. "Hungry?"

"No." I listen to the kitchen clock tick. "I should go pick out an outfit for tomorrow."

As I head for the stairs, Mum shouts after me. "It wasn't your fault either, about Colin…"

Tears sting my eyes as I hurry to the spare room. My cases sit at the foot of the bed, the clothes washed, ironed, and repacked after every use. Each item designer, each item worthless without him.

***

I hop off the bus and hurry towards Hall-In Care's office building as the rain pours down on my freshly washed and styled hair. Trust Mum to need her car just when I could use it most. And trust me to listen when she advised me not to wear a suit jacket because it was 'too fancy'.

Pushing open the glass door, I stand dripping on the doormat, my hair clinging to my face.

A woman about my age, with a sleek blonde bob, looks up. "Can I help you?"

"Hi, I'm Nora McIntyre, I have an interview at ten."

She glances at the wall clock. "You're an hour early."

"I wasn't sure about the buses." I survey the office. Other than the receptionist's desk, there are a few metal filing cabinets and a couple of tub chairs. A small break room is just visible through an open doorway. The two remaining doors are closed, one must be the manager's office. There's no sign of the other applicants.

The woman's frown softens. "How about I show you to the bathroom, let you get dried off." She leads me through one of the unmarked doors.

"I'm Debbie. Give me your blouse, I'll stick it under the dryer for five."

I hesitate before reluctantly handing it over. Mum would be so proud if she knew I'd taken my top off.

Brushing back my sodden hair, I try to regain some semblance of style. It's no good. Less bedraggled bodies have been plucked from the sea. They were probably dryer too, and less wrinkled. Who would hire someone who looks like they swam here? And who has stood in front of their secretary in their underwear. At least I didn't listen to Mum when she told me not to wear a bra 'in case it's a man doing the interviews'.

Karen Brown's words seep into my consciousness. 'You have no experience, no references, and no skills.'

"Here." Debbie hands me a hair bobble.

I wanted to arrive looking keen and professional. Instead, I look like something pulled from a plughole. What idiot doesn't carry an umbrella? My lip quivers.

"Are you all right?"

"I…" I shouldn't have come. I'm lucky they even agreed to interview me. They probably just did it to avoid any later claims of age discrimination. "I'm sorry…" I wipe the tears from my cheek.

Debbie hands me some toilet tissue.

"Thanks. I'm not usually like this. I just really need this job, not that I've any chance of getting it. I don't have any qualifications, not useful ones, anyway. Apparently." I blow my nose. "Sorry, I don't know why I'm telling you all this, but I'm already half-naked so what have I got to lose?" A hysterical laugh escapes my lips. "You seem nice."

That's it, Nora, the ideal first impression, if you were aiming for Babbling Lunatic.

Debbie rubs my arm. "Why don't I put the kettle on? Take five, I'll be in the office when you're ready." She pauses in the doorway. "Mention 'care', 'compassion', and 'kindness', it's the company slogan."

"Thank you." I smile, pulling on my top. "I hope I don't get you in trouble."

She shrugs. "Mrs Hall's all right, just don't tell her I told you." With a wink, she heads back into the office.

Buttoning my blouse, I turn to the mirror and adjust

my make-up. Taking a deep breath, I pull back my shoulders and exit the bathroom.

"Feeling better?" Debbie places two mugs on the desk and takes a seat, gesturing towards the other.

"Yes. And thank you, again."

"Ready?"

I'm not, but I nod anyway.

Debbie smiles, stretching out her hand. "Nice to meet you, Nora. I'm Deborah Hall, the owner and manager of Hall-In Care."

I choke, spitting the tea back into the mug.

"Shall we start the interview?"

CHAPTER THREE

Two months after my rather memorable arrival at Hall-In Care, on a sunny Monday morning, I find myself driving towards Calburn Court, a sheltered housing complex located in the neighbouring town of Calburn.

The development is up a narrow road behind Main Street, and is made up of two rows of white terraced bungalows which flank a garden. At the back of the site sits the main complex where the warden's office is located.

I park Mum's Mini in the private car park and head for the quintet of terraced bungalows on my left.

Skirting the garden, I walk around the buildings to the back where the doors are located. My first solo visit. The client, Mrs Jamesina Marshall, lives at the far end.

The bungalows each have a ramp to the side of the door and a small set of stairs directly in front of it. I opt for the stairs. Chapping lightly, I open the key safe. Empty. Frowning, I try the handle. The door's unlocked.

"Hello? Mrs Marshall?"

Muffled voices talk over each other. A Yorkshire Terrier runs up to welcome me. Bending down, I ruffle his fur and read the nametag which hangs from a tattered tartan collar around his neck. Archibald. The name's bigger than the dog.

Archibald lifts a paw onto my leg. I always wanted a dog but Mum refused. It was the only rule she ever gave me growing up, no dogs. And Colin was allergic, or so he claimed.

The voices rise in volume. Archibald whimpers, scurrying back through a partially open doorway.

Calling again, I walk down the hall and enter what I discover to be the living room. A tall, slim woman in a Ted Baker suit leans over a large, elderly lady in purple pyjamas.

"Listen here you old bat—"

"Careful now." The old woman's voice is firm, commanding.

"Hello?"

The women turn. Scowling, the slim one pushes past me and marches out of the apartment, slamming the door behind her.

I smile apologetically. "Mrs Marshall?"

"No, Mother Teresa." She looks me over in disgust. "I've not seen you before. Aren't you a little old for a new start? With a face like that, you'll be lucky not to be mistaken for a resident."

I do my best to keep smiling while I imagine Mrs Marshall tripping up and flailing back and forth on her bulbous belly.

"I'm Nora, I've come to help you this morning."

She scoffs.

"Shall we head to the bathroom?"

"No, bring a basin through. No point in me marching about the place if I don't need to."

Marching? Chance would be a fine thing. "It's good to walk, helps the bowel."

"I have powders for that."

"Wouldn't you prefer a shower?"

"Wouldn't you prefer to keep your job?"

I think she's warming to me. By the time I'm her age, she'll be dead, and we'll get on famously.

The kitchen is accessed through the living room. It smells of lemon and bleach. The linoleum floor shines, the work surfaces are clear of clutter. Mrs Marshall must have a private cleaner. I certainly can't see her keeping things so spotless.

A large raspberry and chocolate cake sits under a glass dome next to the kettle. My mouth waters. I really should have had a more substantial breakfast, but my nerves got the better of me. All I could manage was a yoghurt.

In the cupboard under the sink, I locate a grey basin. Rinsing it out, I fill it with warm water and return to the living room.

"Do you need a hand to get undressed?"

She affects an Edinburgh accent, mocking me. "Do I look like an invalid?"

You look like a bloated plum.

I lay the basin on the kitchen trolley and position it in front of her.

It still feels rather unnatural to watch someone I don't know getting undressed, so I glance around to make us both feel more comfortable.

Fresh vacuum marks run through the carpet's tread. There are neatly displayed ornaments of dancing girls, but no pictures of loved ones, or mementoes of happier times. Zimmer frames, wheelchairs, and walking sticks sit piled in one corner next to an abandoned toilet frame. The objects look out of place in the otherwise immaculate bungalow.

"I could find out how to get those returned, if you like, give you more space."

"Anything else you want to take from me while you're at it? My Royal Doulton figurines perhaps? To take away any pleasure I have left in my life."

"I'm simply trying to help."

"They all say that then you turn your back and their fingers find your purse. As if it's my fault they didn't finish school and ended up having to degrade themselves."

"I assure you, Mrs Marshall, I'm not like that."

She scoffs. She's good at that, probably considers it exercise.

"Get me cake."

"Sorry?" Did she say 'cake'?

"Are you deaf? Get me cake. It's in the kitchen. You know, the room with the sink and oven. Or didn't you notice those when you were in there? Not very observant are you? I could choke to death and you'd probably carry on chatting."

Her? Choke to death? Chance would be a fine thing. She wouldn't waste the food.

"It's breakfast time, wouldn't you prefer some cereal or toast?"

"Shut up and stop being so argumentative?"

Charming. Still, no point arguing with her, it'll only make things worse. I cut a large slice of the chocolate cake, the crushed raspberry filling oozing out the side. My stomach gurgles.

She's still struggling with the buttons on her pyjama top when I return, but she's managed to open a box of cheap supermarket chocolates. Well, it wouldn't be a balanced breakfast without two forms of chocolate.

"What took you so long? Checking out my silverware, no doubt."

Silverware? More like stainless steel.

I place the cake on the side table next to her. "You've got a hospital appointment tomorrow morning."

"What's that got to do with you?"

"Nothing, I saw it on your wall calendar and was just making sure you knew." I kneel on the floor by her feet.

"I'm not demented." She glares down at me. "Are you some sort of voyeur? Go make yourself useful and get me a drink."

"Certainly, what would you like?" Sherry, perhaps, it is breakfast time after all.

"A bottle of champagne, what do you think you brainless ninny? I want milk, full fat, none of that semi-skimmed nonsense they insist on buying me."

Suppressing an eye roll, I search the fridge. "It's all semi-skimmed, I'm afraid."

"Then use your initiative and add some cream. Do I have to spell everything out for you?"

The last thing she needs is more sugar. Shame I can't sneak some vegetables into it, might do her some good.

When I return, glass in hand, she's still fully dressed in her nightwear.

"Don't just stand there. Help me get this top off."

I'm starting to regret fighting so hard to get this job.

Dutifully, I undo three buttons before my hands are slapped away.

"What are you doing?" Mrs Marshall clutches her pyjama top, pulling it closed.

"You asked for help."

"For help, not to be sexually assaulted."

"What? I would never… I was unbuttoning—"

"You were fondling my breasts. Is that how you get your thrills? Inappropriately touching little old ladies?"

"Little!" Oops.

"Are you calling me fat? Your boss is going to hear about this."

"No, please Mrs Marshall. This is all just a big misunderstanding."

"Big? There you go again with your catty comments."

"No, I…" I pause, composing myself. "I think my intentions have been misunderstood. I'm sorry that I've made you feel—"

"Feel! Vicious girl, making me relive my trauma. I've probably got the PDSA."

It's PTSD, you silly mare. "Please Mrs Marshall, can we talk about this?"

Mrs Marshall attempts to fold her arms over her stomach but can only manage to get hold of one finger of the opposite hand. "I don't want to talk. I want the recipe for this chocolate cake."

She's insane. "You want a cake recipe?"

"Are you deaf as well as stupid? You do understand English, don't you? You certainly don't sound foreign." She glares at me. "Not that that accent's local."

Exhaling, I take my mobile from the pocket of my tunic. "I'll find the recipe online for you."

"Nonsense. Go next door and get it from Mrs Baillie."

"No problem. I'll just be a minute." I'd go to the moon if it'd put an end to this.

"Not now, you stupid girl. When she's asleep."

"I'm sorry?" At least she referred to me as 'girl'. With the way today's going, I'm taking that as a compliment.

"She's not going to just give you her most secret recipe. You're going to have to break into her apartment tonight and steal it."

"I'm not a thief, Mrs Marshall."

"No? So theft is wrong, but feeling up the elderly is all right?" Her mouth curls into a smile.

My stomach tenses, churning bile. She knows I didn't touch her. She made it up just to get a recipe.

I wrap my arms around myself. She's a psychopath.

Leaning back, allowing her pyjama top to gape open, Mrs Marshall runs a finger through the cake's icing and licks it off. "She'll be asleep by ten, I suggest you get there at eleven. I'll be sleeping too, so just post it through my door."

I square my shoulders. "I'll help you get washed, dressed, and give you something to eat. Nothing more."

The cruel smile fades, warmth returns to her arctic gaze. "Oh, fine. Help me get this locket off so I can get a proper wash."

Victory!

Two hours later, I perch on the edge of Mrs Marshall's couch next to Debbie, my leg bouncing with nervous energy. I can't believe this is happening. I should have known she wouldn't let it go.

Mrs Marshall's voice sounds suddenly feeble. "She was

going through my stuff while I was getting dressed. It must have been her who took my locket."

"I wasn't… I didn't."

Archibald shuffles over to lean against my leg. I scratch his back, more for my benefit than his.

"You told me you were going to take my stuff away." Mrs Marshall whimpers.

"The zimmer frames, the stuff you don't use, not… I didn't take your locket." Even the local charity shop wouldn't take it.

"Are you calling me a liar?"

I'd be calling you far worse if I thought anyone would believe me.

Her expression is apprehensive but sincere, her fingers fumble with a wad of tissue. The charade is flawless.

Debbie raises a hand. "I'm sure Nora isn't saying that, Mrs Marshall. Perhaps you put the locket somewhere by accident."

"No, I wear it every day. She insisted I remove it. She said it was so I could get a proper wash. I should have known she was up to something, none of the other girls make me take it off."

Anger rises in my chest. "I am not a thief. I told you that when you asked me to steal a cake recipe from your next-door neighbour."

"Liar!" Her voice booms.

Archibald retreats behind the couch. So much for her weak little victim act.

"Ladies, please." Debbie waits for Mrs Marshall to settle back into her chair before she continues. "These accusations are very serious and will be investigated. If Nora is found guilty, she will be fired."

"She'll be more than fired." Mrs Marshall pops a square of chocolate into her mouth. "She'll be charged."

Debbie looks from me to Mrs Marshall and back. "I'm sure we don't need to involve the police. Not at this stage."

"I already have." Mrs Marshall sneers. "I phoned them this morning, they're coming to interview the pair of you this afternoon."

My lip trembles.

"With all due respect, Mrs Marshall, we haven't ruled out that your locket has simply been misplaced." Debbie's voice is calm. "You won't let us look for it."

"Let a thief rummage through my things. I'm old, not stupid. Goodness knows what else might go missing."

I'm on my feet before I can stop myself. "I didn't take your dumb locket, you stupid old bat!"

The doorbell rings in the silence that follows. Mrs Marshall smirks. "That'll be them."

CHAPTER FOUR

"State your full name for the record."

I lean forward. "Mrs Nora McIntyre."

"Sit back, please." PC Tom Fergusson is mid-forties, with brown eyes and a sneaky smile.

I thought it'd be like it is on television where they interview you in the kitchen, three feet from everyone else, but somehow out of earshot. Instead, I was escorted to Moorbank Police Station in the back of a patrol car, and shown into a beige interview room that smells of vomit.

There is a light knock on the door. A young PC enters and places two plastic cups on the table before exiting. Fergusson moves a hot coffee to one side, out of my reach, and leaves a cup of water in front of me.

"Mrs Hall tells me you've just started at Hall-In Care, where did you work before?"

"I didn't, this is my first job." My first day off of probation and I've already ended up in a police station. I must be more like my mother than I thought.

He glares at me. "You've lived off the dole?"

"No, Colin, my husband, had a good job. He worked and I stayed at home with our daughter, Emma."

"So he made good money?"

"Yes." Didn't I just say that?

He checks his notes. "And yet, when he committed suicide six months ago, he left you with debts of…" His eyebrows rise. "That's quite a figure."

"What does that have to do with Mrs Marshall's locket?" I can't bring myself to mention her other accusation.

PC Fergusson holds up a finger to silence me. "I've been looking into you, Mrs McIntyre. You grew up here, didn't you?"

If you've been doing your homework, you already know the answer to that. "Yes, I moved away when I was eighteen."

"But you'd still know the town well."

"It's grown a lot, but I know most of the landmarks if that's what you mean." Why is he asking me this?

"Your mum, Miss Marian James, is well-known in this town. She must have kept you updated on the local comings and goings over the years."

Well-known, is that police-speak for infamous? "We're not close." PC Fergusson stares at me, so I continue. "We do birthdays, Christmases, that sort of thing."

"But you're back living with her at her property in West Moorland Park?"

I hesitate. "Yes…"

"In fact, your mother paid off a portion of your husband's debts." He inspects his notes. "Sixty-five thousand pounds, to be exact."

"Yes, but I don't see—"

"With money from where?"

"I…" My throat is suddenly dry. Taking a sip of water, I continue. "I never thought to ask."

PC Fergusson interlinks his fingers. "Lots of folk in your family have criminal records, armed robbery, drunk and disorderly, exposure."

"Well, I— Exposure? Who…" Please don't answer that. I picture Mum running naked through the town, chased by policemen brandishing blankets. She would have loved that, she always did like a man in uniform.

"Crime's hardly new to the James clan. A little locket here, a silver picture frame there, nobody would notice. It'd certainly help pay off your debts."

My cheeks flush. "I didn't take the locket." How many times do I have to say that? "I was searched, I didn't have it."

"You could have stashed it somewhere."

"Why would I? It was cheap and battered. Other than giving it to a goldsmith to melt down, its only value was to Mrs Marshall."

"Sounds to me like you gave it a good look over, assessed its value, and even thought about where you could sell it."

"That's not what I said."

"No?" He points to the digital recorder. "I'd be happy to play the tape back." I shake my head and he continues. "Your mum must be proud, a chip off the old block like you…"

I ball my hands into fists under the table. "My Mum isn't a thief, and neither am I."

He smiles. "You're quite defensive of a woman who, in your own words, you're not close to. Perhaps you'd like to amend your statement."

"She's my mother, regardless of the state of our relationship when I was younger."

"Meaning you're closer now?"

My jaw tenses. "This has nothing to do with Mrs Marshall's accusations."

"Accusations?"

My stomach clenches. Does he know about… Why hasn't he mentioned it?

"Mrs McIntyre?"

"The theft."

"You said 'accusations', plural. Has Mrs Marshall accused you of something else?"

I lock eyes with him and shake my head.

"Are you sure?"

I nod, grateful, for once, that Mum's idea of teaching me life skills involved practising a poker face for just such situations. It's a skill I've only used once before when Emma accused me of helping myself to a Twix from her secret stash.

"I didn't steal anything. Mrs Marshall has misplaced it, nothing more."

Fergusson sits back, folding his arms. "Forgive me if I don't take your word for it, Mrs McIntyre."

***

PC Fergusson escorts me back to reception, his hand clamped on my arm as we walk. Pulling open a door, he bundles me through ahead of him.

Debbie is sitting on a blue plastic seat in the reception area. She stands as I approach.

"Don't leave town." Fergusson gives me one final glare before swaggering back behind the scenes.

"That man's been watching too many American police shows."

I attempt a smile.

"I thought you could use a lift." She gestures towards the glass doors and I follow her in silence.

The semi-circular car park belonging to the multi-agency Moorbank Municipal Hub, where Moorbank Police Station is located, is quiet with about a dozen cars strewn across its expanse. This part of town was built after I moved away. It's surprisingly beautiful, with sizeable plots of grass flecked with daffodils and crocuses, and a path leading through the trees to a play park. To my left is a metal bridge leading to Moorbank College. To my right, paths head upwards to the local hospital. Part of me wants to explore, but I don't think I could ever bring myself to come here again.

Debbie unlocks the car. "First time in a police interview room?"

"And my last."

She nods and starts the engine. "With all the questioning, even I was starting to feel guilty."

"I'm no thief." When she doesn't respond, I clear my throat and continue. "This is all just a simple misunderstanding. I'm sure the locket will turn up soon."

Debbie nods, her gaze fixed on the windscreen. "I hope so, Nora." Her thumb taps the steering wheel. "In the meantime, I'm afraid I have to suspend you. Company policy. We have to think of our clients."

No one believes me. No one is going to fight for me. For the first time in my life, I feel truly alone. I keep my head turned to the side, hiding my tears. Why is she doing this to me?

Debbie parks next to Mum's Mini. "Would you mind following me back to the office? There's some paperwork we have to complete."

I nod, there's no point in continuing to plead my innocence, I've already lost. The only person who can figure this out is me. I just have to recollect what happened this morning at Mrs Marshall's. I remember taking off her locket and putting it by the clock on the mantelpiece while she was getting washed. But did she put it back on after? She made such a fuss about everything I was doing — giving her trousers that didn't match her blouse, brushing her hair back instead of parting it to the side — I think I just blocked it out towards the end. As hard as I try, I just can't remember.

And why didn't she tell the police about the other thing? If she wanted to get me in trouble, real trouble, surely that was the way to do it. Or is that still to come?

Parking, I head inside Hall-In Care.

"Take a seat." Debbie tosses her keys onto the desk and heads for the kitchen.

I drop onto the proffered chair, lost in my thoughts. Is

that it? Does Mrs Marshall plan on making further accusations later? But why?

"Here, some decent tea and biscuits." Setting down the tray, Debbie glances at the desk phone. The message light blinks. "Mind if I…" She gestures towards the machine. I shake my head. I'm in no hurry to have Mrs Marshall's accusations added to my file.

"You have five new messages."

That seems excessive.

"Message one: 'Hi Debbie, it's Dan Richards, Muriel's son. Look, I'm sorry to do this, but we heard about the theft, I'm worried about Mum's safety. What's happening? I need to know this has been dealt with.'"

"Message two: 'Hi Debbie, it's Eve Harris. Dad tells me he met this new girl when she was shadowing, he liked her, but… I know you'll have it in hand, just let me know. We'd hate to have to request a different provider.'"

Debbie stops the playback, ignoring the remaining messages. "I could use a stronger drink." Her smile doesn't reach her eyes. "I'm sorry, Nora, really I am, but I have to let you go. The business has only been running for two years, I can't afford to lose clients."

"I didn't do it." My voice is small. Why won't they listen to me?

"I'm sorry, Nora."

I get to my feet, my head bowed.

CHAPTER FIVE

Mum's sunbathing in the front garden when I pull into the drive. She has a back garden. And lives in Scotland. It's barely sixteen degrees, and cloudy. I eye her skimpy green bikini and goose-pimpled flesh. "Is this for Mikey's benefit?"

She chuckles. "He should be so lucky." Her grin turns to a frown as she removes her sunglasses. "You're home early."

Sighing, I head for the kitchen. She follows me inside. "You've been crying."

I fill the kettle and flick the switch.

"Nora?"

I grip the sink. Mum squeezes my shoulder. I turn, throwing myself into her arms. The whole story comes rushing out in between sobs and sniffs. Somehow Mum understands enough to get the gist of what happened. She guides me to a chair.

"That lying cow, as if you'd steal her naff necklace. Has she seen the things in those cases of yours?" She bangs two cups down onto the work surface. "And as for that other stuff... She should be so lucky."

I smile. She believes me. It feels wonderful to have

someone listen, really listen.

Mum busies herself making us a late lunch and keeping my tea topped up. I don't think I've ever drank so much tea before, especially not her tea. But for some reason, today it's helping, and is passably palatable.

She places a plate in front of me and sits down. "So, how are we going to get her to admit she's lying?"

"We don't know that she *is* lying."

Mum stares at me, a forkful of shop-bought potato salad hovering in front of her mouth.

"About the necklace, I mean. The rest of it…" I shake my head. I can't bring myself to think about that. "Maybe she thinks I stole it. Maybe she put it somewhere, or I did, and it's been misplaced. Maybe it'll turn up and all of this will be forgotten."

"That's a lot of 'maybes'." Mum stuffs a cube of Cheddar cheese in her mouth. "But I think it's unlikely. From what you've told me about her, I think she purposely got you in trouble. She wanted you to steal for her and you refused, so she accused you of stealing instead."

I push a stray slice of radish to the side of my plate. "Maybe."

"There's another one. If you're going to do that, you're as well doing it right." I frown and she continues. "Maybe she discredited you as revenge. Maybe she's hoping you'll relent and get that recipe after all. Maybe someone else took her locket. Or maybe she ate it by mistake, you did say she's a big lass."

I laugh. "I don't think she ate it."

"Maybe not." She grins. "Made you laugh though." Mum carries her empty plate to the sink. "So, how are we going to prove that you're innocent?"

"I can't. I'll have to trust the police to do that."

"Nonsense, you've met Fergusson. That man couldn't find a ferret in his trouser leg. Besides, having a criminal record isn't going to help you get a job."

I stare at my plate. She has a point.

"The way I see it, we're going to have to find that locket, and prove your innocence ourselves."

"This isn't one of your cosy mysteries, you're not Miss Marple."

"How about J. B. Fletcher? I've got the right colour hair for that." She pats her long cherry tresses.

Suppressing a smile, I hand her my untouched lunch. "You couldn't write a shopping list, let alone a bestselling crime novel."

"Maybe not. Erotica, on the other hand, now that I could make some serious money from."

I roll my eyes.

"You'll go blind doing that."

"Rolling my eyes?"

"No, eating vegetables. Of course rolling your eyes. It happened to Mrs McGinty's third cousin."

"Everything's happened to Mrs McGinty's third cousin. Her face froze when the wind changed, her nose fell off because she picked it too much, her hands went hairy—"

She sniffs. "She's very unlucky."

"And very made-up."

"Isn't."

"Really? Then how come I've never seen her roaming the streets looking like Quasimodo's uglier sister? Moorbank isn't that big."

"You're never in town. Besides, she only goes out when it's dark. And stop changing the subject, we were talking about clearing your name."

I fill the kettle. "All right, Nancy Drew, what do you suggest I do?"

Mum giggles. "You're a poet."

"And I'm the child here." I go to roll my eyes again but think better of it.

"I think we should break into her house, tie her to a chair, and torture her by eating all her cake right there in front of her. We won't give her any until she confesses."

I place a fresh cup of tea in front of her. "So, to get me out of trouble, you suggest we get ourselves into more trouble. That's insane."

"Och! Fine. Trust the police. Just don't expect me to sneak you cigarettes, those things will kill you."

"You used to smoke."

She waves away my criticism. "That was when it was good for you."

"It was never good for you."

"It was so. Doctors used to advise you to smoke, back in my day."

"That doesn't mean it was good for you."

"You're changing the subject again. We were talking about you rotting in prison where the only job you'll get is as a shiv maker."

I clutch my mug, ignoring her comment. "About the rest… What's she planning?"

Mum places a hand on my shoulder. "Why don't we deal with the lost locket first?"

"Please Mum, I need to know."

She sighs. "She'll let you know soon enough."

"What? But how?"

She sighs again. "The other carers, she'll talk to them about it, get your name. Once she's got that it won't take long for her to get your number."

I drop my head onto the table, wrapping my arms around it. Mum cuddles me. "We're going to get you through this."

We. That sounds good.

"Just promise me that next time you're arrested you'll get legal counsel."

Next time?

She squeezes my shoulder. "Don't worry, I know a guy."

Of course, she does.

**

I shouldn't, it's illegal. But what choice is there?

Something Mum said yesterday kept me up half the night. What if I couldn't trust the police? It's my word against Mrs Marshall's, what if they believe her? What if this doesn't stop at my being accused of theft? I have to do something. Mrs Marshall need never know. She'll be at her hospital appointment. Nobody will think twice about me letting myself in. Why would they? Especially in broad daylight.

My fingers fumble over the key safe numbers.

"Mornin'." The speaker is a boy of about thirteen, with auburn hair. He's wearing mud-spattered jeans and a black t-shirt. Thankfully, Debbie hasn't asked for my uniform back yet, so at least I look the part.

I feign a smile. "Morning."

The boy vanishes around the corner, out of sight. Taking a deep breath, I try the combination again. The key safe falls into my hand, exposing the key.

I can't believe I'm doing this, I must be crazy. Mum would be so proud.

Slipping inside, I give Archibald a clap before heading through the first doorway I come to, the bathroom. It's a small wet room with a cabinet below the sink, and a few wire storage holders.

I search on my hands and knees. Behind the toilet, balanced on the pipe, I find an embroidered lipstick case. Sitting back on my haunches, I open the lid. Curled up inside is a series of trimmed topless pictures of an old man with thinning hair and a moustache. With a shrug, I return the case to its hiding place and continue the search.

Near the shower, the light grey floor is coated in a strange powdery substance which clings to my trousers as I scramble along. The floor feels smoother here, perhaps worn with use. Not that Mrs Marshall seems keen to shower.

I shake the various shampoo bottles as if the locket will

somehow make itself known amongst the thick gloop. Twisting open the lids, I peer inside. Do I have time to pour this out?

You're losing it, Nora. How would the locket get in there?

Unless she dropped it in.

How would she get the lid off with those arthritic hands of hers? What's more, that'd take time and effort, and Mrs Marshall doesn't seem like a lady who would make an effort, except to eat her weight in chocolate.

If she did hide it, where would she put it? Her bedroom?

Archibald stretches and trots along beside me as I march down the hallway. The bed is freshly made, probably by the morning carer. Looks like I'm not the only one who turns a bed down after making it.

On the bedside cabinet sits a china doll in a shabby yellow dress. It seems incongruous. There are so few sentimental items in the apartment. Other than her locket, and the photos in the bathroom, this is the only other personal thing I've seen.

I pick up the doll and examine it. Under the dress, fastened to its waist by an elastic band, is a pendant box. Opening it, I sit on the bed. Inside, perfectly presented on a black foam insert, rests Mrs Marshall's battered locket.

I knew she hid it. As much as I kept telling others that it was a misunderstanding, that the locket was misplaced, I knew. She hid it here, where no one was likely to find it, just to get me in trouble. Well, two can play that game. It's my turn to hide the locket, somewhere Mrs Marshall will never find it, but her carer certainly will. Once it's found and my name is cleared, no one will believe her claims of sexual assault. I'm home free. I'd like to see her try to blackmail me then.

Removing the locket from the box, I head for the kitchen. Pushing open the living room door, I gasp. Staring back at me from the armchair is Mrs Marshall.

CHAPTER SIX

Hand on chest, I step forward. "Oh, Mrs Marshall, you startled me." That's it, Nora, give the game away. I change tack. "Didn't you hear me calling? I came to apologise, I... Mrs Marshall?"

She continues to stare. With another step, I see the cake crumbs stuck to her bulging cheeks, the swollen eyes, and blue lips. Mrs Marshall is dead.

I grab my mobile, then stop. How can I explain my presence here? I could tell them the truth, I haven't done anything wrong. Other than breaking into an old lady's house when I thought she was out. Will they believe me when I tell them it was to find the locket?

I should go, leave her to be found by someone else. No, I can't, no one deserves that. But she wasn't very nice, and that's putting it mildly. They'll find her soon enough.

But what about the locket? I could wipe it down and put it next to her. Some good may as well come from her death. But what if they check it for fingerprints? Won't they be suspicious when they don't find any? But why would they check? They're not likely to carry on their investigations after this, are they?

They might, I was seen entering... No, a carer, a carer

was seen entering. But what if I'm seen leaving? How will I explain not reporting her death?

You're getting carried away, Nora, why would they ask questions? She choked on her own gluttony. Didn't she?

What if it wasn't an accident? What if they think I did it? She did cost me my job.

Stop it, Nora. Who would want to kill an old lady?

Who wouldn't want to kill Mrs Marshall?

Taking a deep breath, I make my decision.

***

"State your full name for the record."

After being escorted to Moorbank Police Station for the second time that week, I'm back with PC Fergusson in the same interview room as before. This time it smells oddly of oranges.

"Mrs Nora McIntyre."

"And Matty Pender, her legal counsel." Mr Pender is scrawny with glasses, uncombed hair, and a crumpled suit. He was recommended by Mum but I have my doubts.

"What will happen to Archibald?" I know the question is irrelevant, but I'm not ready to go through another police interview. Not yet.

Fergusson frowns. "Who?"

"Mrs Marshall's dog."

He rolls his eyes. "Are you planning to plead insanity, Mrs McIntyre? No? Then I think we have more pressing matters to discuss. Like what you were doing in Mrs Marshall's residence."

I swallow. "I was trying to prove I didn't take the locket."

"By breaking into her bungalow?"

"By finding it for her. I thought if she had it back, she'd drop the complaint."

"How do we know you weren't breaking in to recover the locket from where you stashed it? Or to steal more jewellery?"

He has a point.

"Well, I… I suppose you don't… But I wasn't, I wouldn't…"

Shouldn't Mr Pender be saying something? He could at least look like he's paying attention. I make eyes at him, and he grins and winks in response.

"Say something." I hiss.

"Sorry?" He removes an earphone from the ear furthest from me.

Fantastic!

Fergusson scoffs. "For the sake of the official record, Mr Pender has now ceased listening to…" He gestures at him.

"The footy."

I groan. Why did I take a recommendation from my mother?

The policeman smiles. "Good match?"

"Terrible, we're getting thrashed. Your team's in the lead."

Fergusson chuckles. "Do you have anything else to add, for the tape?"

"Yes, your team is a bunch of injury-faking pillocks."

"About the case, Mr Pender." Fergusson glares a warning.

I'm going to jail. I'm going to jail and it's all Mum's fault. Mum's and Matty Pender's. I'm going to jail and I'll never get to wear nice clothes again. What will Emma say? She'll be mortified when she finds out.

"You've given your opening remarks?" Mr Pender asks. Fergusson nods.

"Ah, good. I hate those."

Why does Mum hate me? She must do to land me with this… I lean forward. "I want a new solicitor, a real one, not this… lunatic." It's the nicest thing I can think to say.

"Calm down." Mr Pender pats my knee. He's almost young enough to be my son. Almost.

"I know what I'm doing." He adds.

I doubt that. What kind of solicitor is named 'Matty'? A cheap one, I bet. That's probably why Mum recommended him. I thought it might have been because he was good. More fool me.

Clearing his throat, Mr Pender straightens his suit. The wrinkles remain. "It's a defence of mental disorder now, not insanity. That was abolished as a special defence by section 171 of the—"

"Thank you, Mr Pender." Fergusson looks annoyed. "Anything else?"

"Actually, yes." Mr Pender sits back, looking smug. "Corpus delicti."

Corpse. That was something about a corpse. A delicious corpse? No, that can't be right. "I'm sorry? I don't…"

Pender idly wipes his glasses with his shirt tail. "He hasn't proven corpus delicti."

Fergusson sighs. "You're not in court now, Mr Pender. Plain language will suffice."

"It means the body of the crime."

I frown at him, awaiting a further explanation, which he duly provides.

"A person cannot be convicted of a crime until it has been proven that a crime has been committed. In this case, PC Fergusson must prove that you, Mrs Nora McIntyre, stole Mrs Jamesina Marshall's necklace, and he hasn't. The locket was found in the deceased's residence when the police arrived. They have no proof that it was ever removed from said property."

Oh, he's good. I take it back, I love you, Mum.

"Your client was found inside the property, holding a stolen locket."

"Supposedly stolen," I add.

Mr Pender grins his approval. "Not bad, if you ever want a job—"

"Your client could have brought the locket with her

when she broke into the deceased's property. Or she could have recovered it from where she hid it."

"I already explained—"

Mr Pender cuts me off. "In law, doubtful things should be interpreted in the best way. Unless you can prove that my client took the locket, we must assume that her intentions, when she gained access to the property, were good."

Fergusson leans forward. "When she gained access to the property wearing a carer's uniform. Can you explain that, Mrs McIntyre?"

Not without incriminating myself further. "I…" I may as well put the noose around my neck. "I thought it'd look—"

"Don't answer that." Mr Pender interjects. "My client did not steal the uniform, it was given to her."

It was… Before I lost my job.

He continues. "She doesn't have to explain her… atypical choice of clothing."

That's one way to put it.

"My client caused no damage gaining entry. At most, you have enough to prove that she entered the deceased's property unbidden."

Why did he just point that out?

"Assuming, of course, that Mrs McIntyre did indeed enter the property without first gaining consent." He glances at me. I nod and he continues. "Which you have no evidence of, due to the resident being deceased."

Fergusson sits back, folding his arms. "I don't care about the necklace."

"You don't?" My shoulders relax.

"I don't."

"So, I'm free to go?"

"Not exactly." He sits, silently staring at me.

Why isn't he speaking? Should I say something? Should Mr Pender? You'd think being the daughter of a petty criminal, I'd be more knowledgeable about how such proceedings work.

Finally, PC Fergusson speaks. "Mrs Marshall was murdered."

I gasp. "Murdered? How? When?"

Mr Pender looks as confused as I am.

"She was suffocated sometime last night. Someone stuffed her mouth full of cake and then covered her nose and mouth until she died. We even have proof of corpus delicti, which should satisfy you, Mr Pender."

My brain fills with static.

Fergusson opens a file and places a photograph on the table. Mrs Marshall's swollen eyes stare back at me. I turn away. My words come out in a whisper. "Who would do such a thing?"

He smirks. "I was hoping you could tell me that."

"Me? I don't know."

"Are you sure?" He pushes the picture closer. "Where were you last night from eight PM until midnight?"

"At Mum's house."

"For the sake of the tape, let it be known that the accused's mother is one Miss Marian James who resides at West Moorland Park. Mrs McIntyre, can your mother corroborate your alibi?"

Alibi? "No, she had Zumba."

"Until midnight?"

"I didn't ask."

Mr Pender's Adam's apple bobs as he swallows, his mouth remains firmly closed.

"Nothing to add, Mr Pender?" Fergusson looks smug.

Mr Pender slumps in his chair, looking impassive. "Don't be so stupid, Fergie. What, you think she murdered someone, then returned to the scene of the crime the next morning to phone you? That wouldn't make her a very smart murderess now, would it? Is that PC, murderess?"

I stare at him, willing him to transform back into the legal dynamo he was a second ago.

"Perhaps your client left something behind and

retraced her steps to recover it. After being seen entering said property, your client had no choice but to report her crime."

That sounds worryingly plausible, even to me.

"Said property. Now who thinks they're in court? And can you prove any of this? Was there a witness that saw Nora entering the property?"

Yes.

"We are interviewing residents and staff."

"Meaning there is no witness." Mr Pender picks at his teeth with a fingernail.

"Meaning, our enquiries are ongoing."

What will happen when they find that boy?

"Even if my client did leave something at the scene of the crime, she has justifiable cause for it being there. Because she was there. She was there to assist Mrs Marshall with personal care yesterday morning, as you well know." Pender takes a file from his bag. "In her previous statement, my client reports that she assisted the deceased to undress, and gave her a slice of chocolate cake, at the deceased's request. Mrs McIntyre was in close proximity to the murder weapon at the bidding of the deceased." He closes the file. "In short, you're havering and you know it."

Stop taunting him, you crazy stick insect.

"The deceased accused your client of theft and cost her her job. That's motive. Your client knew the deceased's key safe combination as evidenced this morning when she used it to gain access for dubious reasons. That's means. And she could have done so last night while her mother was… otherwise engaged. That's opportunity."

Means, motive, opportunity. I may not be a detective, but even I know that isn't good.

Fergusson continues. "You may be right, Mr Pender, I might not be able to charge your client with theft but it certainly looks like I could soon be charging her with murder."

Murder. Tears sting my eyes. This can't be happening.

Mr Pender sighs. "If my client murdered Mrs Marshall, why did she return to the scene of the crime this morning? You haven't given a justifiable reason for that."

He shrugs. "There doesn't need to be a 'justifiable reason'. Most murderers are surprisingly stupid."

"They must be for you to catch them."

Wonderful, more taunting. At this rate, I won't be the only one going getting locked up.

"Are you calling me thick, Mr Pender?"

Pender picks up his mobile and idly scrolls. "Well, if you have to ask…"

"Mr Pender, I could have you charged—"

"With what? Hurting your feelings?" He places his feet on the interview table and leans back in his chair.

I was right the first time, the man's a lunatic.

"Tread lightly, Mr Pender."

"Are we back in the courtroom? You're no judge, Fergie, just a beat cop. And I use the term loosely. Are you even allowed to investigate murders? Surely that's a CID thing." He replaces his earphone.

Fergusson's jaw tightens. "Mr Pender, unless you plan on spending a night in one of our cells, I suggest—"

"Come on Fergie, we both know you can't make this stick." He lowers his feet. "No jury will believe my client killed a virtual stranger for a battered locket she'd be lucky to get a few quid for. And murdering Mrs Marshall was hardly going to get her reemployed. It's the shoddiest motive I've ever heard. But then, you do have a track record for that sort of thing, don't you?" He pushes his glasses up his nose, his gaze fixed on Fergusson. "Do you really want a repeat of the Brown Affair?"

Fergusson stands, leaning over the table. "You're on thin ice, Pender."

"Meaning if I continue my bacon will be cooked?" He chuckles, elbowing me in the ribs. "Fergie here once tried to bring charges against Harry Brown, the butcher, because he offered him bac—"

Fergusson's chair is thrown back. He leaps over the table and grabs Mr Pender. I scream, pushing myself away from them. The door is flung open. Fergusson turns, then blanches. "Sir." He relaxes his grip on Mr Pender's collar.

CHAPTER SEVEN

I stand outside Moorbank Police Station, unsure how I came to be released. After relinquishing his hold on Mr Pender's collar, PC Fergusson and Mr Pender left the interview room and a few minutes later an officer arrived and told me I was free to go.

"Enjoying your freedom?" Mr Pender walks over, his hands stuffed deep in his pockets. It's almost certainly a bad idea to slap him while standing outside a police station. Nevertheless, it is very tempting.

A taxi pulls up, Mum climbs out and hurries over. "Nora, thank heavens. Are you all right?"

I nod, and glare at Mr Pender. "No thanks to him. Were you trying to get me hanged?" Or yourself beaten to a pulp?

He grins. "They haven't had the death penalty in Scotland since 1965."

Perhaps I could throttle him and pass it off as a firm hug.

Pender's gaze follows Mum's taxi as it pulls out onto the street. "Actually, I was trying to get you out without Fergie pressing charges. And you're welcome." He straightens his tie and tucks in his shirt. "The murder threw me a bit, had to change tack. Give a lad a heads up next time."

Mum's eyes widen. "Murder? What murder? Nora?"

I shake my head, unsure where to start. Mr Pender comes to my rescue. "The victim was one Mrs Jamesina Marshall, the same individual who accused Nora of theft."

"But they can't think Nora… Matty…"

He gives her shoulder a light squeeze. "Relax Marian, I've got this. Nora's out, isn't she? Took a bit of doing right enough. Fergie got pretty close to messing me up this time."

"This time?" I stare at him. "You mean you antagonised him on purpose?"

Mum chuckles. "Matty's one of the best, cheap too."

I knew he was cheap. Still, he did get me released. For now. I look him over. "How are you with indecent exposure?"

He grins. "Excellent, but I prefer cash."

Heat rushes to my cheeks. "I didn't mean… I… Never mind."

"Smart, isn't he? Cute too." Mum winks.

"I…" There are no words. "Let's go home."

"Fine, where's the car?"

I wince. "It's at Calburn Court."

"Don't worry, we'll get it." Mum plants a kiss on Mr Pender's cheek. "Thanks again, Matty."

"Anytime. See you Friday." Giving a two-finger military salute, he bids us farewell, heading over the bridge towards Moorbank College.

Mum gestures in the direction of the main road. "Let's head for the vets. Don't want to give the gossips something to blether about."

And getting a taxi to the police station won't have started rumours?

"What's happening on Friday?" I instantly regret asking. I've probably just made myself an accessory.

"A meeting of the Moorbank Art Club."

Thank goodness. "Sounds like fun, I might come along sometime." It might take my mind off this whole murder business.

"I didn't know you were into life drawing."

Life… Is that nudes? Indecent exposure, indeed. Dear lord, does he… Does she…

I shudder. "I might give it a miss."

"Shame, we're always after new models. It's very liberating. And they pay." Mum nudges me and laughs. "A little extra money couldn't hurt." She puts her arm through mine. "If you'd rather do the painting, it's a good place to see lots of big—"

"Mrs McIntyre?"

Thank goodness for that, I dread to think what she was going to say next.

The man is wearing a smart suit. He's late forties with a kind smile and a little extra weight around the middle.

"More police?" Mum groans. "She just got out."

He produces a warrant card. "I'm DI Buchanan. May I have a word?"

Mum steps between us. "Without a solicitor? Surely you know better than that, Dic-tective." She emphasises the first syllable.

Antagonising police officers appears to be a popular pastime in Moorbank. It's a wonder Moorbank Sheriff Court isn't busier.

"I'm happy to speak with you." If only to prevent you from arresting my mad mother.

"Careful." Mum hisses. With a warning glare at Buchanan, she steps aside.

"How can I help?" I ask.

"A fellow officer informed me that you witnessed a regrettable incident between PC Fergusson and one Matthew Pender. I wish to apologise on behalf of the Moorbank Police Department, and assure you that the matter will be dealt with."

"What incident?" Mum asks, stepping forward. He

ignores her, his gaze remains fixed on me.

I'm not sure what to say. "Thank you." Why is he apologising to me? Surely it's Mr Pender he should be speaking with.

With a polite nod, he heads back into the station. Mum exhales, fanning herself. "He's a bit of a dish, for a policeman."

I shake my head. Does she ever think of anything else?

Reaching the road, I press the button at the crossing.

"I have to ask…" She indicates my clothes.

Please don't make me explain.

"Can I borrow these?"

That wasn't the question I was expecting. It was far worse. "They're going back to Debbie the first chance I get."

"Shame."

We cross the road and turn right, walking along the grass verge. The road is quiet, with only the odd car passing by.

"So, what now? After we get my car back, I mean."

"Now, I go back to the Job Centre and start again. After all, everybody wants to employ a convicted murderer."

"You think they'll charge you then?"

Given that I seem to have the means, motive, and opportunity…

"Yes." And I don't think Mr Pender's going to find it so easy to have me released next time.

Reaching the vets, Mum phones for a taxi. "They'll be here in five. Look sad, like your cat died or something."

That shouldn't be too difficult.

"Okay, a little less sad, you don't want to scare them off."

Thanks, Mum.

My phone beeps. "It's Emma. What would she think if she knew? She'd never imagine I'd end up in the back of a police car, let alone twice in one week."

"Rite of passage that. In my day it wasn't a good night out without a ride in a cop car."

I feign surprise. "You've been in a police car?"

"Course. Lots of times. I even borrowed one once. Crashed it into that bridge on Market Street."

"The one with the crumbling bit?"

"The very same. Stupid place for a bridge."

"What, over water?"

She harrumphs.

"I can't believe you've never told me that before. What else don't I know about you?"

"Well, don't go round telling everyone, but…" She looks around dramatically. The car park is empty save for a handful of cars. "I'm not a real redhead."

I snort. "You don't say."

A grey Honda pulls in and stops beside us. The driver lowers the window. "Taxi for Ivona Carr?"

"That's us." Mum clambers inside.

Of course, it is. Still, at least her alias is wholesome, for once. "Calburn Court please."

Mum settles back, ignoring the seatbelt. "I don't think scurrying back to the Job Centre's the answer."

"What? Oh, that. I was being sarcastic." And not subtly.

"I think we should solve this murder."

The driver turns the radio down just a fraction. I make eyes at Mum.

"Think about it, it's the only way to prove you're— Are you having a stroke?"

Understated as ever, Mother. "The driver." I mouth.

"Why aren't you speaking? You *are* having a stroke. Really, Nora. What a time to have a stroke. Don't we have enough to deal with already?"

"The driver." I hiss.

"The driver's having a stroke?" Mum squeezes between the seats, grabbing hold of his arm. He bats her away, inadvertently steering into the right-hand lane, before swerving back to the left.

Mum sits back. "Are you sure he's having a stroke? He can't half wave those arms about."

"I never said… I was trying to tell you that he was listening."

She tuts. "We could have crashed. Trust you to get your signals wrong. Honestly, Nora, I've never known anyone to attract as much trouble as you."

Signals? My blank expression must convey my confusion.

"You pull your ear for listening. Everyone knows that."

Clearly not everyone. What are the other signals? Poking yourself in the eye if someone's watching? Breaking wind if something smells fishy?

"So we're agreed?"

I frown. "About the signals?"

Her shake of the head is almost piteous. "About investigating. Think about it, it's the only way to guarantee to prove your innocence."

"That's absurd."

"As absurd as a badger chasing a haggis."

That is quite absurd.

"We can't trust the police to put the right person in prison. Miscarriages of justice happen all the time." Mum nods vigorously. "And okay, sure, so you would get a good amount of compensation after they clear you and let you back out… Actually, that's not a bad idea. Maybe we shouldn't investigate."

"I'm not going to prison just to get compensation. And I'm not risking more police scrutiny by playing detective again either. Goodness knows what I might be charged with next."

Mum takes her mobile from her jacket pocket.

"Who are you phoning?"

"Matty of course." She rolls her eyes.

"You'll go blind doing that." I grin. I've been waiting for the chance to say that.

47

"Thanks for the warning."

It's no fun if she's going to take it seriously.

Switching to the speaker, Mum fills Mr Pender in on the discussion. The driver clicks the radio off. It won't be long before the whole town knows what she's planning.

There's amusement in Mr Pender's voice when he responds. "I'm afraid the legal fees would surpass any reparation gained from a miscarriage of justice."

"Hmm… Okay, crime-solving it is." Mum takes a notebook and pen from her handbag. "We need a list of suspects."

"Just be careful, Marian. The police don't take kindly to civilians playing detective. I'd advise you to keep your investigations within the law. Nora might not be released so easily next time."

Mum and I exchange worried glances.

"Any idea where to start, Matty?" She taps the pen against her chin. "Who normally kills people?"

"Murderers," I say with a shrug.

Mr Pender's response is a little more helpful. "Spouses. Or inheriting relatives. Sheltered housing's not cheap. Assuming her fees aren't being covered by the council, her family could have a motive."

"That, and Nora says she was horrid."

He laughs. "I'm not sure that's a valid motive for murder. However, if you two are serious about this, I'd say they should definitely be on your suspect list. Might be worth tracking them down and ascertaining whether they have an alibi. Assuming she has family, that is."

Mum ends the call, before turning back to me. "So, suspects…" She stares into space. "Do we have any suspects?"

"Well, until we know if Mrs Marshall has a family I guess…" I draw a blank. "Just me."

She scribbles a note.

"I was joking."

"We need to start somewhere. So, what's your

motive?"

"Well, PC Fergusson didn't seem to know about…" I gesture.

"Her saying you climbed the mountain without asking the shepherd?"

The driver glances round.

"His theory…" I continue. "Is that Mrs Marshall discovered I'd stolen her locket, reported me to the police, and cost me my job."

Mum's eyes narrow. "That is a good motive."

"It's not a motive. I didn't do it, remember?"

"I wouldn't blame you if you had."

"Mum!"

"I'm kidding… Sort of. Anyone else?"

I think back to the previous day. "Well, when I arrived at hers yesterday morning, she was yelling at a woman in a designer suit."

"Who was she?"

I shrug. "I'm not sure, a staff member, maybe. Why?"

"Because she's just been promoted from employee to suspect."

I'm not sure that's a promotion.

"And I know exactly how we're going to find out her motive." Mum grins.

That can't be good.

CHAPTER EIGHT

Why did I let my mother talk me into this? It's idiotic. No sane person would come up with a plan that involves two wigs and a borrowed wheelchair. And don't get me started on her choice of outfit, the skirt of which I'm quite sure is a curtain held shut by several kilt pins. Why exactly my mother has a collection of those I'm too scared to ask. Mainly because I fear she'll tell me the answer.

Perhaps this is what she wears every Wednesday for one of those social groups of hers. Wild Women in Wigs, or Crazy Curtain-Wearing Weightlifters, or some such nonsense.

I wheeze, pushing the wheelchair along Main Street in the direction of Calburn Court. Who knew these things were so heavy? "Are you sure about this?"

"It's the only way to ask questions without them getting suspicious." Mum re-applies her lipstick.

"Who's 'them'?" And why would they ever be suspicious of two women wearing wigs?

She scoffs. "Them the staff. We can't have them recognising you."

"I've been there twice, and never in the main complex."

She points to the top of a lamppost. "I bet they'd recognise you."

A semi-circular CCTV camera sits nestled next to the light.

"If they think we're up to something, they'll report us. If they report us, PC Fergusson will check the footage and ID us."

"Who would ever suspect two clowns of being up to something? It's far less suspicious than a mother and daughter visiting a sheltered housing complex."

"Wheesht, you!" She crosses her arms. "Clowns indeed. It's not as if I covered you in white makeup and slapped a red nose on your face. Besides, wigs are very vogue."

I somehow manage to avoid bringing up the hideous outfit she tried to have me wear. Instead, I pull forward a strand of the long wig she forced onto my head half an hour earlier. "Even pink wigs?"

"It's rosé."

"That's pink."

She sniffs. "It's posh pink. There's a difference."

I'm quite confident there isn't. She could have at least let us drive part-way. Instead, I'm left pushing this rickety wheelchair through the town. She refused to walk too, said it'd 'look odd', my pushing an empty wheelchair around. I did explain that they can fold up.

Reaching the corner, I turn the chair, inadvertently propelling Mum into a wall.

"Careful! Mrs McGinty's husband needs this back in one piece. He can't walk, not since his stroke."

Where have they abandoned poor Mr McGinty? I envisage him lying on his stomach on the couch, having been unceremoniously tipped out of his wheelchair.

"It won't turn." I groan.

"Mrs McGinty manages to turn it, and she's seventy-six."

"Good for her." The woman must be built like Arnold Schwarzenegger. Either that or Mr McGinty's a lot lighter than Mum. I decide against sharing my thoughts.

Pulling it backwards, I over-steer, the wheelchair moves towards the road.

"Stop!" Mum clutches her chest. "You're going to get me killed."

"Chance would be a fine thing." My feet slip as I struggle to control the weight.

"Do you want me to get out?"

"What?" Oh, now she's willing to walk. "No, that'd be even more suspicious." I stand in front of the wheelchair, my hands on the armrests as I reposition it and reattempt the turn.

"I'm getting out."

"Don't get out," I growl.

"You're doing it all wrong, Nora. Let me push it."

"Do not get out of the chair."

"Don't damage it."

"I'm not going to damage it."

We're drawing quite a crowd. They probably think it's some sort of performance theatre. Perhaps I should start selling tickets. I could use the money.

"You're steering towards the wall again."

"No, I'm not."

"I'm getting out."

"Do not get out of the chair." I snarl.

"We should have brought the car."

"You wouldn't let us bring the car. You said it'd look suspicious." The words escape through gritted teeth. "I even suggested parking at the bottom of the hill, but you said no."

Mum waves away my comments.

With some assistance from a passing postman, we complete a seven-point turn and finally round the corner. There is a smattering of confused applause from the onlookers. I don't think they enjoyed the show.

"Here we go." Mum rubs her hands together as Calburn Court comes into view. Rain patters against us as we negotiate the surprisingly steep descending ramp, and make our way through the garden to the main complex.

The roses and hydrangea are yet to bud, but the crocuses and daffodils add colour to the otherwise green expanse.

I stop by the external doors. "Are you sure about this? We can't get into trouble, can we?"

Mum pats my hand. "As you said, we're just a mother and daughter taking a tour, nothing more."

I nod and press the push pad. The glass door swings inwards, and a second door slides open.

The wheelchair rattles over the metal threshold onto the ribbed industrial carpet. I trip. Momentum propels me forward. The wheelchair slips from my grip and shoots through the second door and into the narrow hallway, heading for the wall.

Mum yells, covering her face.

With delicate fingers, a smartly-dressed woman stops the wheelchair and glares at me.

It's her, the woman I saw arguing with Mrs Marshall.

CHAPTER NINE

The woman scowls. "You should be more careful."

"And you should eat more burgers." Mum prods her in the stomach.

The slim woman glares at her. "Excuse me?"

I hurry forward. "Nothing."

"Nothing?" She folds her arms.

"Sorry about Mum. She's bad with dementia." I feign an apologetic smile.

"Bad with the men?" Mum sounds genuinely offended. "I'll have you know I've ridden many a stallion in my day."

An embarrassed giggle escapes my lips. "We're here to meet Barbara."

"Ms Veitch."

"Yes, her."

"Me." She looks me over with distaste. "You must be Mrs Troy and Mrs Barnaby."

Who?

"Giddy up, Troy." Mum slaps my haunch.

I can't believe I let her talk me into this. Troy and Barnaby indeed. As if anyone would believe that.

"Shall we?" Veitch steps aside, gesturing for us to follow.

Then again…

Directing us to the left, past a closed door marked 'Warden's Office', she leads us along a magnolia hallway towards a brown door.

"This flat is currently vacant."

I pull the wheelchair backwards, positioning it for the turn.

Clunk. The wheelchair collides with the doorframe. I wince. Mum glares up at me.

The front wheel looks a bit wonky. Maybe it was always like that.

"Shall I?" Without waiting for a response, Ms Veitch commandeers the wheelchair, expertly steering it into the room. She makes it looks easy. She must have excellent upper body strength. Certainly strength enough to pack Mrs Marshall's mouth full of cake and suffocate her. And Veitch and Mrs Marshall were arguing the day before she died. It all makes sense. She killed Mrs Marshall.

Vacant flat. She's showing us a vacant flat. No witnesses.

I step back.

The wheelchair. She has Mum. I need to warn her.

A lump builds in my throat as I reluctantly follow them into the living room.

"This is an example of our single apartment. The residents are encouraged to personalise them, make them more… homely."

"Homely?" Mum scowls. "Vile, more like."

Veitch's head whips around at an alarming rate. If we weren't in danger before, we certainly are now.

Admittedly, Mum's not wrong. The room is a muddy brown, with grey leather seats, and nesting tables from the 1960s. I don't want to die in this room. From the smell of it, somebody already has.

I cough, trying to get Mum's attention. She ignores me and peers out of the window.

"The view is dreadful. Who wants to look at a boring

patch of grass?"

The view is of the garden we walked through earlier. Forget crocuses, Mum would rather have some living statues. Male, of course, scantily clad. What she's more likely to get is clubbed over the head and buried under the roses.

Veitch's eyes narrow. "That *patch* of grass is our residents' garden. You're welcome to ask our gardener, Master Ritchie, to assist you to add some plants of your own."

"Master Ritchie?" Mum chuckles. "Is he a lord? How much land does he own? Or is it just that scrawny wee bit out there?"

Hopefully she'll irritate Ms Veitch enough that Veitch murders her first. Right now, I honestly wouldn't blame her.

"The gardener is unmarried, therefore he is *Master* Ritchie," Veitch explains.

Mum affects an accent worthy of the queen herself. "Oh, how terribly posh. Does he assist one with the walking of one's corgis if one were to make such a request?"

More importantly, does he assist one with the dismemberment of nosy women wearing curtains?

"We don't allow pets. If you wish to reside here, I suggest you have your corgis rehomed."

I frown, thinking of Archibald. "Does that go for the terraced bungalows too?"

"No pets, anywhere."

"But what about—" Stop talking, Nora.

Ms Veitch glares at me. A flicker of recognition crosses her face. She knows I was there, knows I saw her arguing with Mrs Marshall.

I turn away, suddenly fascinated by the carpet. It's covered in burnt orange swirls. Why was that ever the fashion?

Mum harrumphs. "One was not aware of the protocol,

royal or otherwise. One is rather fond of one's canine companions, however, if one must do without... Lead on, Ms Beitch."

Veitch's head whips around again. How does she move like that? She must have permanent whiplash.

"It's Veitch."

Mum waves away her comment. "Beitch, Veitch."

Veitch's fingers flex and extend. If I wasn't so sure she was about to pull a slice of cake out of a pocket and suffocate us with it, I'd congratulate myself on remembering something from my college days.

I give a light chuckle, desperately trying to reduce the tension. Veitch stares at me. It feels as if we stand in silence for a full five minutes before she speaks. "I'll show you our residents' café." She strides out of the flat, her arms swinging.

Mum and I exchange relieved glances before we hurry after her. Well, as best we can with the unwieldy wheelchair.

The residents' café turns out to be a cluster of tables fenced off from the main thoroughfare by a wooden trellis. To the left of the tables is a large serving hatch, revealing the kitchen beyond.

"The menu is updated regularly and caters to all dietary requirements." Veitch indicates the laminated cards on a nearby table. "Residents are encouraged to socialise."

An elderly gentleman shuffles past, winking at Mum. Mum giggles, giving a finger wave. The man pouts then licks his lips, my stomach rolls in response. I clear my throat. "This is lovely. Mum would be quite happy here, but I think something a little more private would be best. Perhaps one of the terraced bungalows, I understand one has recently become vacant."

"And how would you know that?" Veitch inspects a knife.

Yes, Nora. How would you know that? Tell the nice lady, before she runs you through with the water-stained implement in her hand. Dull or not, I'm quite sure she could manage it. "The town rumour mill, you know how it is."

It sounds plausible but Veitch looks doubtful.

The hallway next to the café has a few residents mulling around looking bored. It's a rather public place for a murder… I think. And Veitch didn't garrotte us with her bra in the vacant flat, so what harm could asking a few questions do? We've already dented a doorframe.

"Must have been terrible for her family. Did she have a family?" Their full names and addresses would be wonderful. A witness seeing them commit the crime would be better, but I'll take what I can get.

My question is ignored. Instead, Veitch stops a passing cook and wipes the knife on his whites. At least that won't sharpen it.

"The bungalows are rather expensive." She surveys us, mentally hitting us around the head with her true meaning. Thankfully, my clothes are all designer. Mum's, on the other hand… Did I mention the curtain? What about the ridiculous costume jewellery consisting of more chains than the Tour De France and a ring from a Christmas cracker?

"Well, one is fantastically well-endowed." Mum sticks out her chest, enjoying the double entendre. The old lip-licker, who has been scraping a stain from his cardigan, drops his walking stick, gaping at her sizeable assets.

Did she just shake her… endowments? Dear lord, Nora. Get her out of here before she decides to 'socialise' with that old man.

I step closer to Veitch, if nothing else, it might take some of the power out of her thrust when she attempts to stab me. "She isn't kidding about being…" I wince, "Well-endowed."

Veitch's eyes narrow.

"She's a bit like Branson, all tatty jumpers and a bundle in the bank."

She looks from me to Mum, cogs turning, then sighs. Mum gestures towards the front door. "Lead the way, Babs."

Can't she keep her mouth shut, just once?

Veitch's jaw tightens. "Ms Veitch is preferable."

"Hmm? Spinster, eh? You'd best hurry up and land a husband, before your eggs scramble."

Veitch has put down the knife. Unfortunately for Mum, she appears to be contemplating attacking her with a fork, and a dirty one at that. Somehow that makes it worse.

"Mrs Barnaby, your dementia appears to have made you forget your manners."

And the reason why we're here. I'll give you a hint, it's not to wind up this woman.

"Excuse my mum. It's just her sense of humour."

With another sigh, Veitch turns and heads out of the building.

Mum giggles as I propel her out the door. I'm just glad we're getting out of here before she gives that sleazy senior a heart attack.

"Don't you think you're putting it on a bit thick?" I ask.

"You're the one who said I was a few sweeties shy of a poke."

"You're going to get us thrown out." And me thrown in prison for a murder I didn't commit.

"Lighten up, Nora. Nobody died."

Yes, yes they did.

Veitch marches towards the middle of the terraced bungalows. That must be the neighbour Mrs Marshall wanted me to steal the recipe from. What was her name? Mrs Baillie?

The bungalows are probably identical, but as much as I'd hate to go back in there, I think the idea is to get a closer look inside Mrs Marshall's place. I think. Mum was a bit vague on what our objective was in coming here. Other than increasing our non-existent list of suspects.

"What about that one?" I point at Mrs Marshall's apartment.

"They're all the same."

"But that one's on the end, one less noisy neighbour."

Veitch rolls her eyes. I wait for Mum to scold her, to tell her that she'll go blind. But Mum sits in silence. I didn't know she could do that.

"I shouldn't think noisy neighbours are a concern, not on a tour." Veitch opens the key safe and unlocks the door. I adjust my grip on the wheelchair. Do we follow? What harm could it do? Equally, what good can it do?

"Are you coming?" Ms Veitch's voice is sharp, she's clearly not warming to us. Perhaps it's Mum's insults. Or the fake names. Or the wigs. Did I mention the curtain? Putting it like that, I can't say I blame her.

Veitch heads deeper into the apartment. "It's me, Mrs Baillie. Just doing a tour."

She's home. Guilt grips my heart. But I didn't do anything wrong. I didn't steal the recipe, I didn't even try. Perhaps I should have. Maybe then I wouldn't be in this mess.

That doesn't make sense. Mrs Marshall wasn't killed because I didn't steal a cake recipe.

But what if Mrs Baillie knew what Mrs Marshall was planning? She could have heard her plotting through the wall. I think. What if she suffocated Mrs Marshall with the cake to teach her a lesson? We could be in the murderer's house. What if it's a trap? What if she recognises me? What if she's waiting to poison us?

You're getting carried away again, Nora. How on earth would she recognise you? She's hardly likely to have seen you before.

Fine. Just don't drink the tea. Old ladies always offer tea.

Veitch shows us around. The layout is the same as Mrs Marshall's, but the colour scheme is different. Mrs Baillie seems to favour shades of pink. The walls are cotton candy, the carpet coral, and the furniture has been painted fuchsia.

She'll love this wig.

The whole flat smells of freshly baked lemon cake. I lick my lips.

Don't fall for it, Nora. It might be poisoned.

As we're led into the living room, I finally lay eyes on the murderous Mrs Baillie.

"Hello, dearies." The old lady sits in a recliner, smiling. She has the skin of a woman who's enjoyed many summers in the sun. Her hair is set in a curly bob. A pair of round glasses perch on the end of her nose. She looks… harmless.

Veitch does the necessary introductions before herding us through into the kitchen. Cake tins sit unevenly stacked next to the bread bin, flour dusts the floor.

Veitch hovers in the doorway, probably scared she'll put on weight just by being in the vicinity of so much baking paraphernalia.

She hurries us back into the living room. "Mrs Barnaby here is thinking of moving into the complex."

Mrs Baillie gestures at a pink china teapot. "I've just made tea if you'd like some."

No.

Ms Veitch glances at her watch. "No, we're busy."

Thank you, Ms Veitch. You may have just saved our lives.

"Well, I'd love a cup. And some of that lemon drizzle cake too if you don't mind." Mum attempts to self-propel towards the table. I clutch the wheelchair's handles, pinning her in place.

"Mrs Barnaby, I really must insist that we head back." Veitch gestures towards the door. "I have a meeting at eleven."

"Come on, Mum. Time to go."

Mum slaps my hands off the wheelchair. "Nonsense. A chat with a resident is just the thing. I can find out what this place has to offer."

Veitch glares at her. "I can tell you that."

Mum scoffs. "You young…" She looks Ms Veitch up and down, "…ish things have no idea what us oldies want. I'm sure Mrs Baillie won't mind if we stay for a few minutes. We'll show ourselves out after."

Veitch looks back at her watch. "See that you do." Nodding curtly to Mrs Baillie, she leaves.

Wonderful, left alone with a murderess. Hopefully she'll kill Mum first, teach her a lesson for getting us into this mess.

Mrs Baillie chuckles. "Don't mind old sourpuss, she's too busy for anyone."

"Sounds to me like she could use a bit of how's your father." Mum winks.

I grimace.

"I couldn't agree with you more, dear." Mrs Baillie pours three cups of tea. "That's a lovely wig, Mrs Troy. Delightful colour."

I feign a smile and straighten the vibrant monstrosity perched on top of my head. "It's rosé."

"How wonderfully posh."

Mum sticks her tongue out at me before shooting me a warning glare when I roll my eyes. I must stop doing that in front of her.

Mrs Baillie sits back, clasping her cup. "Now, what are you two young things *really* doing here?"

Mum and I glance at each other.

Mrs Baillie taps the side of her head. "I may be old, but there are no barnacles on this brain."

Play it down, Nora. I clear my throat. "I was Mrs Marshall's carer, I… found her…"

"Nora's being coy. She's the prime suspect in Mrs Marshall's murder." Mum sits up straight, a look of pride on her face. *That* she's proud of.

"Really? You don't say." Mrs Baillie cuts the cake.

"Oh, yes. They want to lock her up, but we can't have

that. So we thought we'd figure out who the real killer is."

Thanks, Mum. You just gave her the perfect excuse to murder us next.

"How exciting." Mrs Baillie sips her tea, her glasses steaming up. "So, who are your suspects?"

Mum snatches up a slice of cake. "Well, there's Nora."

"Yes…"

"And Babs Veitch."

"Yes…"

"And… Well, that's it."

Mrs Baillie glances at me before leaning forward. "And she's definitely innocent, is she?"

Mum sighs. "Unfortunately. This time, at least."

"Mum!"

"Well, would it kill you to spice things up a little? I'm not getting any younger."

"You're sixty-eight." It's hardly old.

She ignores me. She's good at that.

Mum ladles sugar into her cup. "What's your real name, Mrs Baillie?"

I wish she'd stop doing that. It makes it sound as though we're in an elaborate spy thriller.

Luckily, Mrs Baillie seems amused by my mother's odd turn of phrase. She chuckles. "It's Isabel, dear."

Mum slurps her tea. "Who'd be on your suspect list, Isabel?"

Other than yourself.

"Well, myself for one, dear."

Is she psychic?

"You?" Mum stuffs cake into her mouth. Let's hope the hospital has the antidote handy. Of course, I'd need to know what poison was used… There weren't any obvious glass vials marked with a skull and cross bones sitting on the kitchen worktops. But there was that white powder… It might not have been flour.

Mrs Baillie nods emphatically. "Oh, yes. She was a horrible woman. She used to put her dog's duties in my garden to upset me. But it didn't work. In fact, it was fantastic for my roses. And it was my cake that was used to… fill her mouth, as it were. Horrible business." Mrs Baillie sips her tea. "She loved my cakes. The raspberry chocolate was her favourite. She was always trying to persuade people to steal the recipe."

"I refused." So there's no reason to kill me.

"Did you, dear? That was nice. I'm afraid as motives go, mine is not very compelling. But at least it gives you an extra name to put on your list." She smiles.

I'm starting to like her.

"Then, as you say, there's Ms Veitch. Mrs Marshall didn't make her life easy, what with all her grandiose demands. Do you know, she even got the final say on the residents' café menu? It was dreadful, all high fat and no vegetables. And, of course, she somehow managed to persuade Ms Veitch to let her have a pet."

"A pet, you don't say," Mum mumbles through a mouthful of cake.

"A Yorkshire Terrier. They're known for being feisty and intelligent, but stubborn." Mrs Baillie chuckles. "Always a favourite of my George. He was a vet, you know."

"Is that right?" Crumbs speckle the carpet at Mum's feet.

Mrs Baillie grins. "I'm glad you're enjoying that, dear."

She certainly is, judging by the detritus pooling by her feet and on her cheeks. Admittedly, it does look like a very tasty cake.

The cake.

"If you and Mrs Marshall didn't get along, why did she have one of your cakes in her kitchen?" Excellent question, Nora.

I stare at her, half expecting her to break down in tears and confess everything. Instead, she just smiles. "It was her birthday on Sunday. I took it over to be nice. I'd hate to think she might have been all alone on a day like that."

My shoulders slump. That sounds plausible. And thoughtful. Not much like a murderer. Or is it murderess?

Don't be fooled, Nora, that's how they get you.

But Mum's still breathing.

Perhaps it's a slow-acting poison. If there is such a thing. Perhaps I should have read up on common poisons last night instead of reading that Nick Spalding novel Mum lent me.

"Where were you on Monday? Mum scowls down at the crumbs. She's probably wondering if she can still eat them.

"Here, alone. No alibi, I'm afraid, dear." Mrs Baillie sighs. "I don't get much company these days, not since my George…" She points to a sepia picture of a young soldier. "And I'm certainly not as mobile as I once was."

"Did you hear anything from next door?" Mum manages to tear her gaze from the floor.

She shakes her head. "The police asked me the same thing. I'm afraid I didn't. I rarely do."

Mum doesn't show any signs of becoming sleepy or turning purple. Perhaps Mrs Baillie isn't trying to poison us after all. That means I can eat the cake!

I lick my lips, eyeing the slice on the plate in front of me. What harm could it do? Other than to my waistline.

Mum downs the remainder of her tea. "Thanks for the refreshments, and the suspect list. We'd best be off."

But…

Mum gathers up the plates. I watch as the moist-looking lemon drizzle cake is moved out of my reach.

Giving our thanks, we show ourselves out. As I close the door, my stomach rumbles. "You could have upset her, questioning her like that."

"If we're going to do this, we'd best do it right. Remember what Matty said about motives and alibis? She has a motive, she said so herself."

"A weak one, she said that too." If you can even call it a motive.

"And she lives next door to the victim. Does that work as a means?"

If that's all it takes to have a means, everyone in the complex has the means. Residents, staff, carers, cleaners, visitors.

"I think we're getting ahead of ourselves. It's a stretch to say that Mrs Baillie has a motive. The dog faeces was good for her roses, and who would kill someone for attempting to steal a recipe?" Admittedly, the raspberry chocolate cake did look delicious.

Mum shakes her head. "She could have been lying. People do, especially during murder investigations."

"And how would you know that? Solved many murders, have you?"

"Course, every day."

"Ones that aren't on TV."

Mum sniffs. "Don't get much chance around here, too sleepy until you came back."

I can't help but laugh. She really is enjoying this. I must admit, it has been good having her here to help.

"Come on, Troy, let's check out those roses."

My shoes scrape against the ramp as I slow the wheelchair's descent. Perhaps I should have let Mum walk, it certainly would have been easier.

I manage to round the building with a five-point turn. An improvement, but I won't be booking my wheelchair driving test just yet.

Surprisingly, the sun is shining in the residents' garden. That's practically unheard of in Scotland. Any more of this and the locals will be stripping to the waist in celebration.

A dark figure crouches by the base of a hydrangea. Tapping Mum on the shoulder, I point. The figure picks something up and scurries from the garden.

"Get after him."

Shoving the wheelchair forwards, I jog along behind it, my hands gripping the handles.

"Oi, you," Mum shouts.

The figure turns.

CHAPTER TEN

The boy stands before us, a blue bucket clasped in his hand.

"You're the lad I saw outside Mrs Marshall's on Monday morning."

Mum sits forward. "Another suspect."

"Suspect?" The boy's voice cracks. "I didn't do anything, well, gardening, I do that, I'm the gardener, I just garden, well, sometimes I do odd jobs, nothing too hard, I don't touch anything electrical, they wouldn't trust me to do that."

Mum's eyes narrow. "He's rambling. Must be guilty."

"Guilty? I'm not guilty, well, okay, maybe I've reset the time on a couple digital clocks, but it's not like I touch the plugs, okay, maybe I changed a fuse or two, but my Dad showed me how, says a man has to be handy."

"What's in the bucket?" Mum tries to snatch it, the boy steps back.

"My tools."

"Nonsense." Mum jumps from the wheelchair, grabbing the bucket. "A trowel, gloves, and one of those mini fork thingies. Tools, just like he said." She shoves it into his abdomen causing him to wince, his arms automatically taking hold. Mum folds her arms. "Who keeps tools in a bucket?"

"Ms Veitch does. She won't let me buy one of those belts to wear them on, says there's no money in the budget, but they're a tenner, there must be a tenner, who doesn't have a tenner? Well, I don't, but most people do."

Mum frowns. "You ever keep anything else in that bucket?"

"Bait, sometimes, for fishing, you know, worms and stuff. I like fishing, not that I catch much, couple trout sometimes, okay, one trout, once."

"What about dog poo? Do you ever keep that in your bucket?" She bends to sniff the pail, her eyes fixed on the boy.

His ears redden. "I… That's no good for fishing. Who are you? Why are you asking me all these questions? And what's with the bad wigs?"

"Bad!" Mum attempts to tower over him. "I'll have you know these are top-of-the-line, salon-quality wigs that were complimented by Mrs Baillie."

I offer an apologetic smile. "We're not interested in the dog-doo in the roses."

"You're not?" The boy relaxes slightly.

"We're not, Master Ritchie. It is Master Ritchie, isn't it?"

He nods. "Yes, no, I dunno about all that master stuff. It's Ryan, really, Ryan Ritchie."

Ignoring Mum's scoff, I continue. "Mrs Marshall was murdered, Ryan, and we want to know by whom."

"Well, it wasn't me, I mean, I dreamt of her dying, anyone who met her would, but I never acted on it, I'm not a psycho, just the gardener. Well, I'm not even really the gardener, but I don't have a garden of my own, we live in a flat, so they let me help out here, keeps me out of trouble. And I mean that, I stay out of trouble, okay, so I might put the odd online bet on for them, but that's not like bad, bad." Ryan sticks a soil-covered finger in his mouth and chews on the nail. His hand shakes. "I don't want any trouble."

I squeeze his arm. "It's all right, Ryan. You're not in trouble."

He wipes his glistening eyes. "Even if I done it? The dog mess, I mean, not the murder. I know it wasn't very nice, but Mrs Marshall wasn't nice, and she had this way of getting you to do what she wanted, whether you wanted to or not. And I didn't want to, I'm not like that, I like Mrs Baillie and the others."

"Others?" Mum grabs hold of his t-shirt. "Who else were you tormenting?"

Ryan jumps back, pulling himself free. I step between them. "Mum, behave."

Muttering under her breath, Mum drops into the wheelchair.

"What else did Mrs Marshall make you do, Ryan?"

Ryan stuffs his hands deep inside his pockets. "She got me to get her things, extra biscuits from the residents' cafe, toilet equipment from dead residents, I know I shouldn't have, it's stealing, and stealing's wrong, but I didn't think it was hurting anyone, they throw out the biscuits if they don't get eaten. Don't know what happens to the equipment when people die, don't think their families want it. The dog mess was the worst thing, nothing else would hurt anyone, and Mrs Baillie was dead nice about it when she found out."

"So, Mrs Baillie knew that it was you who put the dog-doo on the roses?"

He nods. "She said it made them grow better, and it did. Good fertiliser." Ryan indicates a patch of rose bushes. "Mrs Baillie told me to keep doing it, for the roses, and so Mrs Marshall stayed off my back, I don't want trouble, I like it here, sure, my friends tease me for hanging out with a bunch of crinklies, but—"

"I'll show you crinklies, you cheeky little—"

Thankfully, my glare silences Mum, for once.

"Stay here." I stare at her long enough to let her know I'm serious.

Ryan and I walk towards the bench outside the main complex, abandoning Mum.

"Why did you do it?"

Ryan pulls a stray weed from the foot of the bench.

"We're not going to tell anyone, Ryan. We just want to know why you put dog-doo in Mrs Baillie's roses if you like her."

He lowers his head. "I was just gardening, that's what I do. I was going around the bungalows, a few weeks ago, heading for the bits of grass at the front, and heard a noise. I saw someone at the window, figured it was Mrs Marshall moving about, but Mrs Marshall, she said I was watching her get changed, said she'd seen me peek in some of the other windows too. But I didn't, I like old people, but I don't like-like old people, you know. I don't want to see them like that, that creeps me out."

"Well, that bum-fluff you call facial hair isn't all that either, boyo." Mum stands beside the bench, scowling at Ryan. I wave her away. She scoffs, crossing her arms.

Sighing, I continue. "So Mrs Marshall threatened to tell Ms Veitch you were a peeping tom?"

Ryan frowns. "Who's Tom?"

Mum tuts.

"Look, I didn't murder anyone, maybe that Tom bloke did. I just did the dog mess, Mrs Marshall hated Mrs Baillie, dunno why, she's so nice, makes great cakes too."

"Agreed." Mum brushes cake crumbs from her top.

"Who else was Mrs Marshall blackmailing?"

Ryan looks surprised. "I dunno, I thought it was just me."

"Where were you on Monday?" Mum asks.

Did she have to? He's just a kid.

"I was here." He nods in my direction. "You saw me. I went home for tea 'bout five. Mum was working late, Dad took me to the cinema, said I'd earned it." He beams. "I've been doing better in maths, and Dad says that's a good subject to do. We don't get to go out much, we even got popcorn to share. Dad says the extra money from me working here is really helping. Says we might even get to go to the football one day. You won't tell Ms Veitch, will you? I've never been to a match, I don't care who's playing."

I smile. "No, I promise we won't."

"What about after the cinema?" Mum asks.

"We played footy in the garden until ten, then I went to bed."

Mum opens her mouth to continue but I grip her arm, silencing her. My turn to ask the questions. "Do your parents know, about Mrs Marshall blackmailing you?"

He shakes his head.

"That's a lot for you to deal with on your own."

His eyes fill with tears.

"It's over now, Ryan. You're safe." I smile again, trying to reassure him. "Did you see anyone else coming or going from Mrs Marshall's yesterday?"

"Not that I remember, but Mr Marshall visits most days, dunno why."

I frown. "Mr Marshall?"

"Mrs Marshall's son, he called her 'mother', dead creepy that, I'm thirteen and even I don't do that. Then there's Lillian, the cleaner, she's there every day, so I'm sure she would have been in. Lillian cleans for lots of the residents, not as much as she did for Mrs Marshall though. She's real nice, reminds me of my mum."

"Do you know Lillian's surname?" It could prove useful.

Ryan grins and affects a posh accent. "Mrs Lillian Grant, Head of Domestic Services."

Thanking Ryan, we say our goodbyes. Mum is almost giddy with excitement. "We've just solved our first case."

"We have?"

"Of course. The Case of the Dog-doo in the Roses."

I sigh. "Shame we're trying to solve a murder."

"Well, it's not a total loss. We've got two new suspects. Mr Marshall, the son, and most likely heir. And Lillian Grant, who Mrs Marshall was bound to have some dirt on.

"Whom."

Mum continues, ignoring me. "Why else would she clean for her daily?"

That's a good point. She's rather good at this, not that I would tell her that. "Okay Mrs Barnaby, where next?"

"Next, we find Lillian Grant."

We head back inside the complex. This time I manage to negotiate the two sets of doors without tripping. Sadly, nobody applauds my success.

Mum points to the Warden's Office. "I bet that's Veitch's office."

Did I say she was good? I may have given her too much credit.

"She might know where we can find Lillian."

Then again…

The door is closed. Voices are audible within. Mum places a finger to her lips. I nod, pulling the wheelchair out of view of the office window.

I recognise Ms Veitch's voice. "What do you mean, it's over? She's dead."

"I know about Terry." The second speaker is male.

"Terry? What about Terry?"

"Mother saw you, Barbara. There's no point denying it."

"Your mother was a liar, Paul."

Mum grips my arm. "That must be Mrs Marshall's son."

That's quite an assumption. "Mrs Marshall can't be the only person to die, especially not around here, they are old." They probably have the stonemason on speed dial.

"Who else would call their mum 'mother'? Well, other than Norman Bates."

She has a point.

"No, no, no!" An elderly lady is bundled past, struggling in the grip of a woman to whom she bears a strong resemblance.

"It's okay, Mum." The woman rubs her mother's back as she propels her along the corridor.

Mum's eyebrows rise. "You better not be thinking of putting me in a place like this."

I smile. "They wouldn't take you."

"Good."

We lean closer to the door.

"She showed me pictures, Barbara. She couldn't have faked those. She didn't have the technical know-how."

"Then she got someone to do it for her. You know what she was like."

"Yeah, and I know what you're like too. I see the way you leer at other men, I'm not blind."

"No, just weak."

"Careful…"

"Or what?" Veitch continues in a softer tone. "We both know you'll come crawling back. If it wasn't for me, how would you get your thrills? Your wife? She doesn't know what you like."

Whimper.

"What you really like."

Groan.

"She doesn't know what a bad little boy you've been. Does she, Pauly?"

I lean back. "We shouldn't be listening to this."

"Are you kidding? It's just getting good. Very Fifty Shades." Mum attempts to peek through the window.

"How do you know about Fifty Shades?"

"We read it at Smutty Book Club."

"Smu—" No, Nora, you really don't want to know.

Mum glances back at me. "What, would you rather I knitted?"

Yes. "No."

"You sure? Mrs Evans has a pattern for willy warmers.

She made one for her Stan last Christmas."

Please, no.

"It was an elephant with big floppy ears and a surprisingly long—"

"Mum!" Oops.

The office door is thrown open.

CHAPTER ELEVEN

Veitch stands before us. The buttons of her crisp white blouse are undone revealing a white camisole beneath. Behind her stands a fifty-something balding man with a beer gut.

Mum nods in his direction. "Christian."

"Why were you listening at my office door?" Veitch's jaw clenches.

"I… I…" I have further questions. I was looking for the bathroom. "I—"

"I know what you like too, Pauly." Mum winks at the man.

"I… I…" I need to get better at lying. "I didn't want to interrupt."

"What exactly do you think you're interrupting?"

My cheeks flush. "Well, I—"

"Some good old-fashioned rumpy-pumpy." Mum grins.

I close my eyes. Common decency would prevent most people from saying something like that. And then there's my mum. I should be grateful she didn't use a more vulgar expression.

"I'm sorry?" Veitch looms over us, hands on hips, her voice loud.

"We wanted to ask about additional services." The words tumble out.

Her eyes narrow. "Excuse me?"

"Cleaning! I mean." My voice is squeaky. "Nothing else. Certainly nothing untoward. Not that I'm suggesting there's anything wrong with... Not that you were…" Stop babbling, Nora.

"Cleaning can be arranged. For an additional fee."

I sigh, relieved to have been rescued from the grave I was digging for myself. "Excellent. Is the cleaner around? We'd like to speak to her."

"What for?" Veitch asks.

"To borrow a duster, for you to use in your—"

I clamp my hand over Mum's mouth. "My mum's very particular, I want to make sure her standards will be met."

Veitch looks us over then raises an accusatory eyebrow. "Peculiar is more like it. That'd certainly explain the wigs."

With a yell, I pull my hand away, wiping it on my trousers. She licked me. Who does that?

Mum smirks at me before turning to Veitch. "They're very vogue. Especially the pink one."

I thought it was rosé.

Blushing, I remove the hairpiece. Recognition flashes in Veitch's eyes. "I know you."

"Me? No. We should be going." I pull the wheelchair back from the doorway.

"You're the carer. The one I saw at Mrs Marshall's the day she died." She crosses her arms. "Paul, call the police. I think they'd be very interested in knowing you're here, asking to see inside Mrs Marshall's bungalow."

Mum stands, puffing out her chest. "And even more interested to know that Mrs Marshall was blackmailing you."

Paul stops, mid-dial. "Barbara?"

Mum and Veitch lock eyes. They stand at an impasse, Veitch's eyes narrowing, Mum's remaining blank.

Veitch's gaze flicks to the floor. "Forget the police,

Paul."

He frowns. "What? But they—"

"I said forget it." She unfolds her arms. "I want you two to leave. Now. Don't come back."

Mum plonks herself down into the wheelchair. "We'd love to Veitchy-baby, but we've got a murder to solve."

Veitch almost smiles. "You two, detectives? More like Digestives, crumbly and plain."

I feel Mum tense. She looks at Paul, a smile on her face. "We know."

He replaces the receiver. "What is it you think you know?"

She continues to smile and stare. Paul licks his lips. "Look, I don't know what you think you know, but there's nothing to know."

Mum's smile broadens.

"Why would there be? I'm an honest, god-fearing businessman."

An honest, god-fearing businessman who cheats on his wife.

He shifts from foot to foot. "And even if there was, what business is it of yours?"

It was him, he killed her. The babbling, the body language. I've never seen a man look so guilty. It's over. That man will crack in seconds under PC Fergusson's questioning.

Paul wrings his hands together. "Who are you? Did Denny—"

"Shut up, Paul." Veitch steps to the right, blocking Mum's view of Paul, and tags back into the staring contest. How do they do that? My eyes hurt just watching.

Finally, Mum signals me to back away. I do so, reversing the wheelchair as she continues to stare.

With some effort, I haul the wheelchair around and head for the lift. As the doors close, I lean forward. "What do we know?" Were there tell-tale smudges of chocolate on his shirt? Or scratches on his neck?

Mum chuckles. "Nothing, but those two have a lot of badly buried bodies in their basements. People like that are always worried they'll get found out."

"You were bluffing?" I press the button for the top floor, desperate to get as far away from Barbara Veitch as I can. "What if they find out?"

"They won't."

"How do you know?"

"I'm psychic."

"No, you're not."

Mum shrugs. "Might be, you don't know."

I sigh. I do know.

"Stop sighing, Nora. Anyone would think I'd said something stupid."

I roll my eyes. Thankfully, she doesn't see my reaction. The last thing I need is for her to give me another row.

The doors slide open.

"Come on, let's go find that cleaner." She rubs her hands together. She really is enjoying this.

I push her along the corridor in silence, lost in my thoughts.

"So, what do you think?"

I frown. "Sorry?"

"You haven't heard a word I've said. A fine detective you'd make. You're supposed to be aware of the world around you, especially people."

"Sorry. What did you say?"

"Maybe I should interview Lillian alone. I know you're trying, but you're too soft. You weren't happy when I asked Mrs Baillie and Ryan for their alibis. Sometimes you're going to have to ask the hard questions to get the answers you need. No matter how it makes you feel inside."

I'm not soft, not these days. Anyway, how would she know? We've hardly seen each other in the last twenty years, not until Colin…

Clearing my throat, I square my shoulders. "I'll

question Mrs Grant."

Mum doesn't look around, offering only a solitary shrug. I take that as a win.

An elderly gentleman exits his room. I slow the wheelchair, not wanting to startle him. Then recognition strikes. It's the man from before, the one who was hitting on Mum.

He turns away, jingling a set of keys as he searches for the right one. I speed up, my feet slipping on the thin carpet as I hurry to get past before Mum spots him.

"Hey, handsome."

Rats!

Key in lock, the man looks round. A grin spreads over his face, deepening his wrinkles. "Well, hello there, lovely lady. Fancy a tour of my old homestead? It's quite a sight." He winks, licking his lips.

I shudder. He's so slimy.

"Name's Sammy McAllister." He bows theatrically, stumbling slightly as he tries to regain his balance.

Slimy Sammy.

Mum giggles, actually giggles, again. Vomit gurgles up into my mouth, and I choke it down. Sammy pockets his keys and pushes open the door. Saluting, he awaits our entry.

"Onwards, Nora."

I guess that means we're going in. My mind fills with images of silk sheets and velvet walls. I hold my breath. I can't imagine I'm going to enjoy this.

Reluctantly, I try to push the wheelchair forward. It doesn't move. Mum throws me a glare. Giving an apologetic smile, I try again. I know I'm not great with this thing, but I swear it's getting harder to push.

My feet dig into the worn carpet as the wheelchair squeaks and then begins to move. With a hard shove, it bumps over the threshold.

Mum gasps. I stop, staring. Sammy's hallway is nothing like I expected. On the wall facing us is a hand-painted mural of Edinburgh Castle.

"Not bad, eh?" Sammy grins. "There's more inside." He gestures towards an open doorway. From the looks of the lock, it must be the bathroom. I hesitate. Mum scrabbles out of the wheelchair, straightening her... well, curtain, it's a curtain.

Above the cistern is another mural, this time depicting the Scottish Parliament building.

Sammy sniffs. "Best place for that monstrosity."

"Did you paint these?" Mum asks, tilting her head.

Sammy nods. "Self-taught too." If he has braces, he'd be stretching them with smugness.

Maybe I'm being a bit harsh. He really is talented.

Sammy glares at the mural, then licks his lips.

Nope. He's definitely slimy. Maybe he's a suspect. Only one way to find out... "Did you know Mrs Marshall?"

Sammy heads through the open door of his living room and lowers himself down onto a battered old armchair.

He didn't answer my excellent opening question. I bet he did it. I bet Mrs Marshall insulted his art and he snapped. I bet the police find his slimy saliva all over the crime scene.

I follow him. On the wall to the left is a depiction of The Kelpies at nightfall.

Mum bats her eyelids. "You're a very good artist, have you—"

"Getting back to Mrs Marshall... Did you know her?" Ha! Who's asking the tough questions now?

"Lovely lady. She was always doing nice things for others. Can't imagine who would..." He shakes his head.

Mum and I exchange glances. Lovely? Mrs Marshall?

"Jamesina Marshall?" I have to check.

Sammy nods, his eyes glistening with tears. "She gave me this." He holds up his walking stick. "Helped me no end."

I frown. "The equipment in her apartment..."

"She'd get young Ryan to take it from the flats of those

81

who… have moved on. Then she'd give it to others. Nightmare of a time we have trying to get it from the council. Jamesina was kind enough to hide the loot at hers until it was needed."

I clear my throat, biding my time while thinking of a nice way to phrase my next question. "Others didn't… Not everyone thought…" Why am I so bad at this? Composing myself, I try again. "I—"

"We heard she was a cow."

Thanks, Mum. Blunt as ever.

I shoot an apologetic smile at Sammy. "I think what Mum means is—"

"We heard that she was a liar and a blackmailer."

Sammy stares at us, muted by shock.

I laugh nervously. "Forthright as ever, Mother."

"Go make tea. Extra sugar." She leans forward, patting Sammy's knee.

I do as bid, banging the cups down on the work surface. There's a salt shaker next to the teabags. Tempting. But the lady asked for sugar, lots of it. I ladle seven heaped tablespoonfuls into a particularly hideous floral cup before adding three teaspoonfuls to a Hibernian mug.

Placing everything on a tray, I carry them back to the living room.

"Thanks, love." Sammy looks at the weak tea. "Just how I like it." He picks up the floral mug.

"Oh, no, that's actually…"

He slurps loudly.

"I thought the Hibs…"

He smacks his lips before licking them and sighing. "Just how I like it."

Good lord, that tea must be sweeter than candy floss. If that's how he likes it, I doubt any of those teeth are his own.

Mum picks up the Hibernian mug and scowls at the tea. "Did you even use a tea bag?"

I'm going to kill her. I'm going to find the murderer, get some tips, and then I'm going to kill her.

"Yes." I struggle to hide the anger in my voice.

She sips the tea, wincing. "You sure?"

"Yes."

"Doesn't taste like it."

Next time I'm using salt. A whole tub of it.

Mum pours the tea into a nearby plant pot. "So, Mrs Marshall wasn't blackmailing you then?"

Sammy looks up. "Me? What is there to blackmail me about?"

I dread to think.

"She was my… friend."

"As in friend-friend?" Mum looks disappointed.

"Maybe, given time." Sammy wipes his nose with a cloth hanky.

"When did you last see her?" Good question. Well done, Nora. Feel free to pat yourself on the back later.

"Yesterday. She invited me round for cake."

"What time was that?" Another good question. By Jove, I think she's got it. Maybe I can add 'crime-fighting' to my C.V.

"'Bout three. She was thinking 'bout…" Sammy shakes his head and takes a large gulp of tea. "Don't suppose it matters now."

Mum sits forward. "It might matter. Now, more than ever."

Sammy frowns before comprehension spreads over his face. "Oh, but I doubt… I mean, people do, but…"

I smile, trying to reassure him. "Why don't you tell us about it?"

Sammy sighs, staring down at the carpet. "She was thinking 'bout changing her will, giving everything to her son, Paul."

Mum frowns. "He's not the heir?"

Sammy gives a light chuckle. "Doubt you could call anyone that. But he wasn't the beneficiary if that's what you mean."

Mum and I exchange glances.

"Then who is?" She offers Sammy a biscuit.

He shrugs. "Her granddaughter, I suppose. Not that I asked. None of my business that."

"Did Paul know that he wasn't going to inherit?" She helps herself to a Custard Cream.

"Like I said, it's none of my business. Not that I didn't…"

"Didn't what, Sammy?" Mum asks.

Sammy holds out his mug. I hurry to the kitchen to make more tea.

"I advised her against it. I know it weren't my business but… She had her reasons for removing him in the first place. And I was worried about her, see?"

"What reasons?" Mum scowls down at her freshly-poured tea. "Did you add sugar?"

I sigh as Sammy continues. "Paul owns a second-hand car dealership, a right wee earner it is too, but he has a weakness for the ponies. Sunk 50k in one afternoon and expected Jamesina to bail him out. She tried to help, bless her, but there's not much you can do for people like that." Sammy taps his thumb idly against his mug. "Smart girl, that Jamesina, she found a way of stopping them from taking his house."

"How did she do that, Mr…" Don't say slimy, don't say slimy. "Sammy."

"She had him sign his house over to her. Only way to keep it safe."

How long does it take to change a will? If she's already amended it, that'd give Paul Marshall a very good motive for murdering his mother.

Who needs forensics, and close-ups of clues? Just gather a group of gossipy pensioners and you can get all the information you need.

Placing his mug on the table, Sammy excuses himself. Mum and I huddle together, whispering.

"If Paul's that much of a liability, why change the will in his favour?"

Mum nods. "And does the granddaughter know she was about to be disinherited? I smell a motive."

The toilet flushes. I'm not sure it's a motive Mum smells.

Sammy hobbles back to his armchair.

"Why was she changing her will?" I ask.

"And does her granddaughter know?" Mum adds.

Sammy looks startled. He mops his brow before responding. "Sorry ladies, it's all been a bit much today. Do you mind…" He indicates the door.

I wonder if he accepts bribes. Somehow, I doubt my Louis Vuitton handbag is Sammy's style.

I glance at Mum who shrugs.

"Thanks for the tea, Sammy." She gives him a hug before we leave, closing the door behind us.

"I never thought anyone would have something nice to say about Mrs Marshall."

Mum nods, dropping into the wheelchair.

"So, Paul Marshall may a motive to kill his mother."

"Hmm."

Hmm? Is that a 'hmm, you may be onto something', or a 'hmm, you've no idea what you're doing Nora, don't give up the day job'? If only I had one to give up.

I look down at Mum, trying to decode her cryptic response. She's staring at the wall in front of us. It's beige and flat, and boring. Just a wall really, like all the others. I think Sammy's relationship with Mrs Marshall really upset her, lord knows why.

After briefly considering leaving her to brood, and enjoying the silence, I wrap my arms around her shoulders. She pats my hand.

Standing, I scan the deserted corridor. "How are we going to find Lillian? If that's still the plan."

"Course it is. We'll find her, then we're going to track down the granddaughter. We'll leave Paul Marshall for last, let him squirm."

And squirm he would if he knew we were going to be speaking to him again. I'd rather leave Ms Veitch for last. Although, I think it'd take a lot to make her squirm.

I shudder, my thoughts returning to the sounds emanating from behind her closed office door. Oh, how I wish I could whitewash my brain.

"Maybe we should just chap some of these doors, someone's bound to have—"

"Shhh! Listen." Mum looks about furtively. If she was slimmer, she might resemble a meerkat.

I listen. Hard. I'd never noticed how noisy Mum's breathing was before. If she'd just hold her breath for a minute or so… Then I hear it. The faint whir of a vacuum cleaner.

"Follow that sound." Mum points in the general direction of the noise. I brace myself and push. My legs ache, my arms shake. The ancient wheelchair creeps into motion. Either Mum's gaining weight faster than Usain Bolt runs, or something's wrong with this wheelchair.

"Wall!" Mum's shriek brings me out of my thoughts just in time to see the boring, flat, beige wall.

I swerve. The wheelchair stops with a clang and a jolt. Mum buries her head in her hands.

"It's fine, it's fine." I kneel by the wheel. Still wonky. I guess it was too much to hope that the bash would have knocked it straight.

The wall looks a bit more interesting now. It's still beige, but now it's slightly less flat and boring. A chunk of plaster lies on the carpet.

Standing, I push hard, trying to make a clean getaway. The wheelchair gives a low groan but refuses to budge. Growling, I put all my weight into it. Nothing.

I stare down at the wonky front wheel, hoping a clump of plaster is caught in its metalwork. No such luck. Maybe I can straighten it. I glance at the neighbouring wheel. The neighbouring wonky wheel. That can't be good.

"You've broken it, haven't you?"

Maybe someone around here can fix it. This sort of thing must happen all the time. Yes, Nora. The elderly residents regularly propel themselves into walls. It helps to pass the time.

Mum looks down. "I told you to be careful. I told you that Mrs McGinty needs this wheelchair back. And what do you do? You pinball it off every wall you can."

Tears sting my eyes. Mum laughs. I didn't expect that.

"Like mother, like daughter. Me in a cop car colliding with a bridge, and you walloping walls with a wheelchair. What a pair." Getting to her feet, she opens a nearby cupboard door and stuffs the wheelchair inside. "There." She marches off down the corridor, leaving me standing alone in the plaster dust.

CHAPTER TWELVE

"This is insane. We're going to get caught." I don't know why I'm wasting my breath, she's not listening.

Mum pulls open doors at random. It's amazing she hasn't given an unsuspecting resident a stroke. She could at least have the decency to knock first.

"What do you plan to do if you find one? Tip the user out and run?"

She chuckles, clearly enjoying the thought.

"Mum."

"Keep it down. Some thief you'd make."

"That's the point, I'm not a thief. Remember?"

She sighs. "I'm only asking you to keep an eye out."

It's only Wednesday, and so far I've been accused of theft, and murder, and have now been made an accessory by my own mother. Perhaps by Friday, I'll have progressed to GBH.

"What about CCTV?" I search the ceiling for cameras.

Mum vanishes through an unmarked door. There's clunking and banging before she emerges, clutching her prize, a curved plastic stick with a button at one end and an oval of silicon at the other. Whatever that is, it's certainly not a wheelchair.

"Put it back."

"Might come in handy."

"For what?"

She grins. "Come on, this wheelchair won't find itself." Off she walks swinging the stick as she goes.

I scurry after her. "Will you please put that back and stop stealing."

"It's not stealing, not really."

"Taking whatever that is, and a wheelchair without permission is most definitely stealing."

"We left them the other one."

"The broken one."

Mum shoos away my words. "Place like this will have a man to fix it, no problem."

"Then why don't we just find him and get Mrs McGinty's wheelchair fixed ourselves?"

She laughs. "Finding a man is never that easy, not unless you know where to look."

"Since when was finding a man a problem for you? You've already flirted with two today." That I know of.

A smile spreads over her face. That can't be good. I repeat the words in my head. They sound so innocent. To me, anyway.

"Sammy's stick."

I'm almost scared to ask. "What about Sammy's stick?"

"He said he got it from Mrs Marshall."

Oh, no.

"He said she had lots of equipment at her place."

Please, no.

"I bet she has a wheelchair or two."

Don't say it.

"Nobody would notice if we took one. And Sammy did say she kept that stuff to give to others. Others like us."

She said it.

"What about the cleaner? Shouldn't we find her first? Maybe she knows who killed Mrs Marshall. Maybe she did it. Maybe she's disposing of evidence as we speak."

It's no good. Mum trots down the corridor, cupping her endowments, the strange plastic contraption still clasped in her hand. If Sammy could see her now… On second thoughts, let's hope nobody sees her. A sight like that would probably land us with a few more deaths to explain.

Shaking my head, I follow. Within seconds Mum has a fair head start. I lengthen my stride. Her lead increases. I speed up further. Mum rounds a corner out of sight. I break into a slow jog, trying to look inconspicuous. Yes, Nora, because people jog down the corridors all the time here.

An elderly woman backs out of her flat, dragging a zimmer frame. She looks around, her eyes wide. "What's happened, dear? Is it our Mavis? Did she get into the continence cupboard again?"

"No, no, she's fine. I'm just training for… something. Nothing to see here." Just a crazy person chasing an elderly lady down the corridor. And I use the term 'lady' very loosely.

Wait, the continence cupboard? What could happen to someone sneaking into a continence cupboard that causes the staff to run… Jog? And what does she mean 'again'? I desperately want to stop and ask questions but Mum's getting away.

Pushing through a doorway, I enter the stairwell. Two floors below, I spy Mum hopping down the stairs. How the devil does she move so fast? I break into a run, well, as much of a run as I dare. I don't want to beat her to the bottom face first. Then we really would require a wheelchair.

I catch sight of Mum's floral curtain as it vanishes through a fire door on the ground floor. I'm surprised the curtain hasn't made a bid for freedom. And how can she run so fast while wearing it, especially while adopting that ludicrous posture? Perhaps that's the secret to gaining speed. Perhaps top athletes just refuse to do it because they'd look silly. Especially the men.

Glancing around, I cup my modest contribution and hurry after her. I feel ridiculous. I'm quite sure I look ridiculous too. And what's worse, I'm not moving any faster. Then how…

With a groan, I release my grip and slow to a walk. Of course she's fast, she's spent years running from the police. Not for anything major. Not that I know of anyway.

A memory of Mum dashing out of church followed by three burly policemen and the minister flashes through my mind. She'd replaced all the church's wine with diluting juice.

After she fled, one of her exes drove me home. By the time we arrived, Mum was sitting at the kitchen table with the minister and the policemen, all of them sozzled. No charges were brought, and Mum was back at church the following week as though nothing had happened.

I'm huffing and puffing by the time I catch up with her outside Mrs Marshall's house.

Holding the weird plastic thing between her legs, she attempts to break into the key safe.

"No luck? It's not like you. I'd have thought you'd be halfway to the car by now."

She harrumphs. "There are ten thousand possible combinations, these things take time. I've already tried the standard preset code. It'd help if I knew her birthday or wedding anniversary."

Ten thou— That's impressive if she's right. Of course she's right, Nora.

"It's just a matter of—" The key safe drops into her hand. I couldn't have opened it that fast and I know the combination.

Unlocking the door, she steps inside. This is a bad idea, a really bad idea. A 'spend some time in jail' kind of bad idea.

I close the door carefully behind us. Archibald peers around the living room doorway before entering the hall, his tail wagging.

What is he still doing here?

Mum flattens herself against the wall. "Careful Nora, they've got a guard dog." She waves her plastic stick at him.

I kneel, scratching him under the chin. "Archibald's no guard dog."

"True. 'Dog' is a bit strong a word for that hairy rat."

Archibald climbs into my arms and I stand.

"Put that walking rug down. It's probably riddled."

Shaking my head, I carry him to the kitchen in search of food. Mum hovers behind us. "I bet he did it."

"Who, the dog? Don't be daft."

"He probably crawled up on her to get a heat, and lay on her face."

"Nonsense. Archibald wouldn't hurt a fly."

"It's not the flies I'm worried about."

Rolling my eyes, I put Archibald down next to his food bowl, and sniff. No suspicious smells. Someone's been looking after him.

Mum retreats into the living room, making a beeline for the equipment piled up under the window. She inspects a wheelchair, propelling it in small doughnuts around the room. She's positively beaming. "This'll do nicely."

"Good, then let's get out of here."

We head into the hallway. Maybe it'll be okay, maybe we'll get away with it.

A key clicks in the lock.

Mum throws herself against me, propelling both of us into the bedroom door which remains stubbornly shut.

The front door opens.

"What are *you* doing here?"

It can't be.

CHAPTER THIRTEEN

"I said, what are you doing here?"

Mum steps back, releasing me. I straighten my wig. "Well?"

"I could ask you the same thing, Karen."

"It's Miss Brown."

"Oh, no it's not. Not here."

Mum looks from me to Karen and back. "Friend or foe?"

We answer simultaneously. "Foe."

"This is Karen…" The professional harpy. "From the Job Centre."

Mum frowns. "The jumped-up wee madam?"

Karen flicks her blonde hair over one shoulder. "I'm a recruitment consultant, actually."

That's not what I'd call her.

"So? What are you doing here? And what's with that stupid wig?"

Why is it always about my wig? Mum's wearing one too.

Mum squares her shoulders. "It's rosé."

"My mistake, I didn't realise rosé was French for stupid."

Mum points her plastic stick at her. "It's posh pink."

"It's very vogue," I add, not sure it'll defuse the situation. But then, Karen could do with a slap, and I'd love to be there to see it.

"I'm calling the police." Karen takes her mobile from her pocket.

"Good." No, Nora. Not good, not good at all. "Then you can explain to them what you're doing here."

She pauses. "What I'm doing here? In my grandma's house?"

Her grand— I don't know why I'm surprised. They're like two cacti in a terrarium. "You're the granddaughter?"

"And you're the prime suspect." Karen pouts. "What, did a little hard work turn out to be too tough after all? Still, you lasted longer than I expected. Guess I owe Jackie a fiver."

"You bet I'd fail?"

She smiles. "Pretty safe bet, as it turns out."

If Mum doesn't hit her, I will. Hard. Okay, so I'll probably miss and land flat on my face, but I can try.

Wait, Karen Brown, not Marshall?

"Where were you on Monday?" Mum's question startles me.

Karen's eyes narrow. "What's it to you?"

"My Nora's in the frame for this."

"Are you sure she's innocent?"

Why does everyone keep asking that?

Mum nods, lowering her plastic stick. "She is. This time."

Thanks, I think.

Karen crosses her arms. "What's it worth?"

"For your alibi, or for not calling the cops?"

"Both."

Are they really doing this? Somehow I don't think Karen will accept the assorted coins Mum has to offer. I'm not even sure they're still legal tender.

Mum pulls up her sleeve revealing a gold watch.

"Vintage Rolex."

Where did she get that? Other than from up her sleeve, of course.

Karen quirks an eyebrow. "I'm listening."

"This watch for your alibi, silence, and this wheelchair."

"And Archibald," I add.

Mum and Karen stare at me as though just realising I'm still here.

Karen turns back to Mum. "That watch for my silence and the wheelchair, nothing else."

They lock eyes. My shoulders relax. Mum's got her now.

Mum looks away. "Deal."

What? But Mum never loses when it comes to a staring contest.

Unclasping the watch, she tosses it to Karen.

"What about Archibald?" I ask.

Karen stares down at the watch. "Who?"

"Him." I scoop the small dog up into my arms.

"That flea-ridden mutt? You can have him for free, saves me paying that boy to feed him."

That boy? Ryan. So that's who's been looking after him.

"Saves me a trip to the rehoming centre, too." Karen scowls at the Terrier as if he just piddled in her Prada purse. "I say the rehoming centre, I mean the lay-by off junction five."

I hate her, I really hate her. But, wait… "Why is he still here? Surely Forensics…"

Karen sighs, her eyes roaming the limited furniture and paintings in the narrow hallway. "His hair was already everywhere, I mean, seriously." She glares down at her shoes, checking for the slightest bit of fur. "And what's-his-name wasn't allowed to take him home, something about the rules of their rental." Her disgust is clear. Imagine having to live in a rented property.

Karen fixes her gaze on me, the look of disgust remains. "Anything else?"

"Yes." Mum pulls at her finger. "I'll give you my ring if you take that walking hairpiece back."

"No deal," I growl.

She harrumphs. "Fine, fine, he can come."

Dropping Archibald onto the wheelchair I gather up his bed and toys. Arms full, I march towards the front door. "Mum, grab the wheelchair." I shove Karen aside. Sadly, she barely registers the impact. I wish Mum had hit her.

A sudden shriek makes me turn. Karen hops up and down clutching her ankle. "Watch it with that thing."

"Don't be such a baby, it barely touched you." Mum realigns the wheelchair and aims for Karen's other leg.

Karen leaps out of the way, clattering into the sideboard.

"They're harder to steer than they look. Here…" Mum hands her the plastic stick.

"What is it?"

"A bum wiper."

Karen squeals, dropping the contraption.

"I know there's already a stick up yours, so I knew you'd like it." Chuckling, Mum wheels Archibald towards the car.

I dread to think what she was planning to do with that thing if we hadn't met Karen.

***

"She's the murderer. She has to be." I pace back and forth in Mum's kitchen, Archibald trotting along behind me.

"What's her motive?" Mum asks.

"She doesn't need one, she's just pure evil."

She chuckles. "I'm not sure even Matty could make *that* stand up in court."

"Well, okay. Maybe Mrs Marshall was blackmailing her."

"Blackmailing her own granddaughter? About what?"

"Who cares?"

"PC Fergusson, the judge, the jury…"

"She's sleeping with her boss."

Mum sits up straighter. "Is she? How do you know? Did you see something juicy?"

"She must be. She looks the type."

"Nora, I'm surprised at you." Mum takes the lid off the biscuit tin. "That sounds more like something I'd say." Crumbs drop onto the table as she continues. "Besides, without evidence, it's just speculation."

I stop and stare at her. "That's a big word."

She huffs. "I can use big words."

"But you used it properly."

"I can do that too."

I frown. "Law and Order?"

She takes another bite of her biscuit. "It's not from a TV show."

I continue to stare.

"It's from that Word of the Day calendar you got me for Christmas."

Now I'm really surprised. "You kept that?"

"Of course, why wouldn't I?"

"And you use it?"

She rifles through the biscuits. "It's surprising, I know, but even I can work a calendar."

I look meaningfully at the kitchen wall. Mum follows my gaze. "I've been meaning to change that."

"For three months?"

She sniffs. "You live here too, you could have changed it."

I'm not that brave.

"Shall I?" I lift the calendar off the wall.

"Depends. What's the pic?"

"Another half-naked fireman."

"Does he have a big hose?" Mum titters.

I sigh, closing my eyes. "Am I changing this?"

"Go on then. It's a good one that, got it from Mrs McGinty's old man."

Who gives their wife's friend a racy calendar for Christmas? On second thoughts, I don't want to know.

"I can't believe you gave her your watch."

Mum waves away my comment. "It was nothing."

"It was a vintage Rolex."

She shrugs. "It was certainly vintage." A smile spreads across her face.

My eyes widen. "It's fake?"

"Got it at the Barras back in '71. Old George Mackie was a dab hand at reproductions." She places the biscuits aside. "Okay, back to the matter at hand. I think we should go over what we know so far."

I nod. "Sounds good. What do we know?"

We sit in silence. Surely we know something. Anything.

I sigh. I would have been better spending the day picking out an outfit for court.

"I've got it." Mum jumps to her feet and hurries from the room.

Boxes clatter, a cupboard door slams, and then footsteps approach. Mum enters carrying a whiteboard and a marker.

"Where did you get that from?"

She frowns. "From my room. Just now." She indicates the door.

"No, I mean… Forget it. What's it for?"

Mum grins. Pulling the lid from the pen with her teeth, she begins drawing lines. Should I tell her she's just streaked her cheek? Maybe later.

She lowers the board, looking triumphant. There's now a four-column grid with 'suspects' on the left and…

"MOO?"

"Yes, you know, their motives and… chances to do it, and ways to do it, and stuff."

"You mean, 'MMO', not 'MOO'."

Mum scoffs. "Potato, tomato."

"No, it's…" Why bother, Nora? I sigh again. "Okay, what's next?"

"Next, we add the suspects." She begins scribbling, her handwriting barely legible. Finished, she looks up, awaiting praise.

"Looks good."

She grins.

"Just one question."

Her eyes narrow. "Look, 'MOO' is close enough. If you're going to start being picky…"

"No, it's not that."

"Go on then." She's still looking at me suspiciously.

"Why is my name on there?"

Her look changes to one of pity. "Well, Nora, dear, you are a suspect."

I think I just lost my eyebrows in my hairline. "A suspect I think we can rule out. Especially given that we both know I didn't do it." I'm almost shouting by the end.

"So you say, but you do have an excellent motive."

"Mum!"

She chuckles. "All right, all right. Look, if we include you—"

"Despite my complete and unquestionable innocence."

"Yes, ignoring that, then we can find evidence that you can't have murdered Mrs Marshall."

"Evidence of innocence? Is that a thing?"

She shrugs. "Who knows? But it should be. Then, we can be one step ahead of Fergusson the next time he comes to question you."

She has a point. A good point. A very good point.

"All right, let's figure this thing out."

There's a soft munching and crunching. Archibald stands on the chair, his front paws on the table, his head buried in the biscuit tin.

Mum glares at me. I scoop him up and lock him in the

living room before she starts taking dog care tips from Karen Brown.

Ten minutes later, the board is almost as bare as before, only now, my reasons to kill Mrs Marshall are clear for all to see. I swear Mum's taken to standing that little bit further away. She's been eyeing the knife drawer too. Can't say I blame her, even *I'm* starting to doubt my innocence.

Is it possible to murder someone and have no memory of doing it? Maybe I should check the washing basket for bloodstained clothing.

"Okay, so we've got you—"

"Who we are discounting."

"Who we are discounting. Then there's that boy Ryan, who I think we can discount too."

"Why?" Did I miss something?

Mum scratches her cheek with the back of the marker pen. "Because, well, he's too stupid to murder anyone."

Wait, that's not—

"Then there's Sammy, who we can discount straight off because, well, there's no motive."

"That we know of."

She glares at me. "There's no motive, Nora."

So, Slimy Sammy's not a viable suspect but I am? Fantastic.

I concede with a small nod, there's no point arguing with her when she's like this. "What about Mrs Baillie?"

She shakes her head. "That sweet old thing? She wouldn't harm anyone."

"Even she said she should be added to the suspect list."

She snorts. "Because of a cake? That's hardly a motive."

Not like mine. "I still think we should add her."

Mum sighs and reluctantly adds the name. "It's still a very flimsy motive, Nora."

I'm not so sure about that. When I was twelve, I saw Mum stab someone in the side with a fork for the last slice of pizza. If she can do that, surely cake can be a motive.

Mum continues. "Then there's Ms Veitch. We know Mrs Marshall had something juicy on her. How else did she get all those extra services Mrs Baillie told us about?"

I nod. "She's my top suspect, right after Karen Brown."

"Hmm, I don't know. Mrs Marshall was a big lass, Veitch is all skin and bones."

"Did you see how easily she pushed you around in that wheelchair? She's stronger than she looks."

Reluctantly, Mum agrees. "We still need to find out where she and Paul Marshall were on Monday."

"And where Lillian Grant was."

"Yep, got her."

I frown at the scribble. I wondered what that said.

"So, what have we got?" Mum stands back.

We stare at the board.

"Nothing." I lower my gaze.

Mum clicks the lid onto the pen. "All right, let's sleep on it and start afresh tomorrow."

Nothing.

My hands tremble. I hadn't realised how much this detective nonsense had distracted me from my impending imprisonment.

Mum heads for the cereal cupboard. From a box of out-of-date, overly sugared wheat flakes, she pulls a large bar of chocolate. Breaking off a square, she offers it to me. I shake my head. Some things chocolate can't fix.

CHAPTER FOURTEEN

The next morning, I'm greeted by the scent and gentle sizzle of bacon. Mum's already dressed. A mountain of sausage and egg sits on the kitchen table. Archibald stands by Mum's feet, licking his lips.

"Morning." She plates up the bacon. "There's fresh tea in the pot."

I glance at the clock. Eight AM. This is bad. This is very bad.

I hover in the doorway. "What's happened?"

"Nothing. Sit, eat."

I don't move.

"Sit, sit."

Nope.

Mum lowers the frying pan. "Okay, there is something. But it's a good something. I was speaking to Mrs McGinty last night when I went round to return her wheelchair."

That wasn't her wheelchair. That was a dead person's wheelchair, stolen from the house of another dead person.

"And I asked her if she knew Lillian Grant."

I approach the table. "And?"

"And, she does."

I sit. "And?"

"And she told me where to find her."

We would have found her yesterday if Mum hadn't deviated from our plan. Okay, so my crashing the wheelchair into a wall and breaking it may have had a little something to do with it. But she was the one calling the shots. Speaking of which... "When are we going?"

"Straight after this."

I look at the mound of food. After this, it'll be a quick heart attack and a trip to A&E before we go anywhere else.

Adding a slice of bacon to my plate, I remove the fat. Mum spears it with her fork and drops it into her mouth. Grease dribbles down her chin. Maybe I should get dressed so I'm ready to take her to the hospital.

"Eat up, bird-belly." She bites into a sausage. "Sleep all right?"

I shake my head.

"Maybe you'll feel better after a shower."

Smiling, I carry my tea toward the bathroom.

Mum's right, the shower does help. Afterwards, I take Archibald for a walk and in no time, Mum and I are driving towards town.

"So, where are we headed?"

Mum continues to stare at the road.

"Mum?"

Nothing.

"Where are we going?" My voice is firm.

She sighs. "The Moorpond."

"The... Is that a good idea?"

"Why wouldn't it be?"

Because the last thing I need is you sloshed, sobbing, and singing show tunes. "I'm just surprised. It's a bit early for a drink is all."

She doesn't answer. Maybe it won't be so bad. Maybe they're not open yet. Lillian might clean for them, too.

The Moorpond is your traditional tatty, tired pub with a few rooms to rent. It sits in the middle of a wooded area, with no pond in sight. The only water anywhere near there comes from a tap.

We pull into the car park at the side of the pub. Despite the bitter bite in the air, a few hardy patrons sit on benches in the beer garden. If you can call a strip of green-streaked mud a garden.

"How will we find her?"

"How do you think? We ask." Mum heads straight for the bar.

The barman smiles as we approach. "Morning, Marian. The usual?"

"A large one. And the same for Nora, here."

"Make that two teas, please."

Mum glares at me. "Speak for yourself."

I drag her away. "Don't do this. You've barely got your one-year chip."

She pulls her arm free of my grasp. "My usual, Freddie."

Freddie nods.

Plastic cracks, bubbles hiss. Freddie places the drink on the counter. I stare at the bottle of coke. Still glaring at me, Mum snatches it up. "Thanks, Freddie."

The barman grunts, pouring hot water into a metal teapot. Mum takes a large gulp of her soft drink before leaning forward on the bar counter. "Do you know a Lillian Grant?"

Freddie runs a cloth around the inside of a glass. "Might do."

"Is she here?"

"Might be."

"What does she look like?"

Freddie inspects the glass. "Can't say I've noticed particularly."

"You must have noticed something." Mum pays for the drinks.

He shrugs. "Female. Wears clothes. Has hair. The usual."

"Anything unusual?"

Freddie returns the now-clean glass to the pile.

Mum slaps the bar. "Fine. You win. No strip spades in the back room for one month."

The barman smiles. "Table by the window, short, plump, late-thirties, rosy cheeks, short brown hair streaked with grey, and a nervous giggle."

With a curt nod, Mum heads in search of the illusive Lillian. I trot after her.

"It's three-year chip."

I frown. "Sorry?"

She stops suddenly causing me to bump into her. Thankfully, the tea remains in its pot.

"I'm three years sober, not one. And I have no intention of having a drink now."

"That's…" Fantastic. Inspirational. The right words fail me. "Sorry."

She smiles. "Me too."

"But what about strip spades?"

Mum waves away the question. "I said we wouldn't play in the back room, I never said anything about out here."

I laugh. Trust Mum to find a loophole. I must ask her what night she plays strip spades, and make sure I avoid the bar at all costs.

We spot Lillian easily. She sits alone, a bag of cheese and onion crisps on the table in front of her. With a few gestures towards the vacant chairs, she signals for us to join. She's exactly as Freddie described and reminds me of the type of mother I'd wished for when I was growing up, instead of the motorbike-riding groupie I ended up with.

I picture Mum, early forties, in her black snakeskin miniskirt, sneaking gulps from her hipflask, and singing saucy lyrics to traditional songs. It was certainly a memorable Christening. Goodness knows what possessed them to make her the godmother.

Still, I wouldn't change her now, not for anything.

Lillian's giggle brings me out of my reminiscences.

"Me? I didn't clean Mrs Marshall's on Monday."

"But the place was immaculate." I point out.

Well, except for the bathroom floor. I frown, remembering the strange powdery substance that had clung to my knees. What was that? I hadn't dared try to get it off, instead burying the trousers in the washing basket, hoping they'd somehow clean themselves.

Mum helps herself to one of Lillian's crisps. "Ryan Ritchie told us you clean her house every day."

"And there were fresh vacuum marks in the carpet," I add.

Lillian shrugs. "Must have been from Sunday." She moves her crisps further away from Mum.

"And her walking about didn't disturb them?" Mum gulps her drink.

"Mrs Marshall didn't walk about. She just sat in that chair and ate chocolate."

She has a point.

"Where were you on Monday?" Mum draws the crisp bag back to her side of the table.

"What time?"

Mum and I look at each other. What was it PC Fergusson said? Eight PM?

Regretfully, I shrug at Mum, she shrugs back and turns to Lillian who is clutching the packet of crisps. Mum looks disheartened. Lillian gives an apologetic smile but continues to grip her prize.

"From noon until midnight," Mum says with another shrug.

Midnight. There was something about midnight.

Lillian responds instantly. "Noon 'til four I clean at Calburn Court, but not Mrs Marshall's. Then from four 'til six, I was at home. Six 'til eight I was at Hall-In Care, then home to bath the bairn and get him to bed. I was there the rest of the night."

"Can anyone co-oberate that?" Mum signals Freddie

who throws her over a packet of crisps.

I lean towards Mum and whisper, "Corroborate."

She tuts. "That's what I said."

Lillian blinks rapidly before giggling. "Just the bairn, which is no good unless you speak three-year-old. I'm afraid it's all Bing Bunny, and Baby Shark."

Thanking Lillian we head back to the car.

"Well, at least we can strike her from the suspect list."

Mum scoffs. "Nonsense. Did you hear how quickly she told us where she was on Monday? I can't remember where I was yesterday, let alone four days ago."

I'm not sure she should admit that. Certainly not out loud.

I shrug. "She has regular clients."

"Could be. Or, more likely, Mrs Lillian Grant has been rehearsing her answer."

"Or PC Fergusson already questioned her, so it's fresh in her mind."

"For the whole night? Mind the police will have a far clearer time of death to work with."

So would we, if only I could remember. What was it PC Fergusson said? Was it eight? It could have been eleven. Or five, for all I know. There was something about midnight though. Maybe Mr Pender would remember.

I suddenly realise that we're still in the pub car park. The engine remains quiet. Mum scrabbles through her handbag.

"What are you doing?"

She pulls out her mobile. "Phoning Matty, see if he can give us more info on the time of death." She puts the phone on speaker.

Mr Pender answers on the third ring. "Marian, if you're phoning about strip spades, Freddie already phoned."

Life drawing, strip spades, I'm starting to think these two are made for each other.

"Forget about strip spades, Matty. This is an official call."

"Should I put my tie back on?"

"And your trousers," Mum says with a giggle.

"Spoilsport."

I want to vomit.

Mum waits a few seconds before continuing. "Trousers on?"

"Trousers on." Mr Pender says sulkily.

"Okay, down to business." Mum takes her notepad from her handbag. "We need an accurate time of death for Mrs Marshall. Any idea, Matty?"

"Sometime between eight and midnight."

Eight, I was right.

Mr Pender continues. "They might have a more accurate time by now. But if they have, they're not sharing."

Mum scribbles a note. "Thanks, Matty."

"Can I take my trousers back off now?"

"Only if you leave the tie on."

I attempt to snatch the phone from Mum's hand, she bats me away. Mr Pender laughs and ends the call.

Mum starts the engine. "Hall-In's down on Smith Street, isn't it?"

"Yes, why?"

She pulls out of the car park. "Why do you think? To check Lillian's alibi."

I groan. The last place I want to go is back to Hall-In Care. Correction, the last place I want to go is prison.

CHAPTER FIFTEEN

Debbie is unsurprisingly surprised to see me as we push open the door and enter the offices of Hall-In Care. I smile as she jumps up from behind her desk and hurries forward.

"Nora, I wasn't expecting..." She looks at Mum. "Who's this?"

"Marian James." Mum offers her hand. Debbie hesitates before taking it.

"She's my Mum," I add, making sure she knows I've not been rounding up old people to provide care for.

Debbie's smile looks more genuine now, and my shoulders relax.

"I thought the name sounded familiar."

Mum grins. She looks thrilled that I've told Debbie about her. Except, I *know* I haven't.

My stomach sinks. However she knows my mother's name, it's not likely to be good.

Debbie proffers a chair. "What can I do for you?"

I perch on the edge of the seat.

"I'll cut to the chase. Nora needs your help."

"Why don't I put the kettle on? I have a feeling I'm going to need it." Debbie excuses herself and soon returns with the familiar tray. "So… How can I help?" She pours three cups of tea.

"Nora didn't kill Mrs Marshall." Mum rummages through the plate of biscuits as though hoping to find a Jammy Dodger hidden under a Digestive. "We're trying to clear her name."

"Okay…"

"We need more information on Mrs Marshall."

Debbie frowns. "What kind of information?"

"Right now?" Mum settles for a Ginger Nut and dunks it in her tea. "Whatever we can get."

"I'm sorry, it's confidential. My business would fold if anyone found out."

I lower my gaze.

"How about some…" Mum circles her now-soggy biscuit in the air. "Unofficial information?"

Debbie's eyes narrow. "For example?"

"Who do you think would want to kill her?"

"Unofficially?" Debbie gives a sheepish grin. "Anyone who met her."

Mum chuckles. "That's a given. Anyone in particular?"

"Possibly her niece, Karen. I don't have anything to base that on, she's just a piece of work."

I smile. I knew I liked this woman. We could have been friends, if I hadn't been accused of theft and murder, and tarnished the name of her care agency. Guess that's what she gets for taking a chance on me.

Tears sting my eyes, I clear my throat.

Debbie leans forward. "Look, if you want information you'll need a solicitor, a good one. Even then…"

Mum produces Mr Pender's card and slides it across the desk. The card is covered in illegible scribbles. She must give him a lot of business.

Debbie's eyes widen. She drums her fingers on the desk before pushing back her chair and taking a thin folder from the filing cabinet.

"You didn't hear any of this from me, understood?"

We nod.

"Mrs Marshall has been with us for about a year now, ever since her last care agency refused to support her. She received care twice a day—"

"Twice?" Mum sits forward in her chair. "What time was the second call?"

Debbie opens the file. "It's a tuck call, scheduled for between six and ten."

"And she got that care on Monday night?"

Debbie checks her computer. "Yes, the carer logged in at nine-fifteen, and out twenty minutes later."

Mum helps herself to another biscuit. "So, she was alive at nine-fifteen?"

Debbie blinks several times before responding. "Yes. I'm quite sure if she wasn't, it would have been noted here."

"And her AM call on Tuesday, were they running late?"

Good question. They should have been there before I arrived, so why didn't they find the body? If they had, none of this would have happened. Well, I may have been spotted wandering around in a uniform I had no business wearing. But compared to this…

"Mrs Marshall cancelled the visit. She had an early hospital appointment, and since we couldn't guarantee the time of the visit…"

"How was she getting to her appointment?" Mum asks.

"Her son usually drove her."

"So why didn't he find the body?" Mum's in full interrogation mode now.

Debbie frowns. "I… I don't know. You'd have to ask him."

"Have you got his details?" Mum reaches for the file.

Debbie snatches it up, holding it out of her reach. "I do, but I can't give them to you." She looks at me apologetically.

"What about this?" Mum waggles the business card in front of Debbie's face.

"My nephew's card will only get you so much."

Matty Pender is her nephew. That must be how she's heard Mum's name before.

Even Mum seems surprised by the revelation. "You're Matty's aunt?"

"And you're his best client."

Thankfully, Debbie looks more amused than annoyed as Mum continues. "What's the name of the carer who visited Mrs Marshall on Monday night?"

Debbie shakes her head. "That's a confidence too far."

Mum slumps back in the chair.

"Lillian Grant!" My voice is louder than intended.

"Yes, Lillian Grant." Mum sits up. "Was she here on Monday night?"

"Lillian? Yes, of course. She's here every Monday."

Mum drops back again. "That's that then."

Giving our thanks, we head to the door.

"Wait a minute." Debbie stands. "Lillian wasn't here on Monday. She was supposed to be, but she never showed. I remember because I stayed late to document..." She blushes, avoiding my eye.

Mum steps towards her desk. "What time did you leave?"

"About ten."

"Could Lillian have been here after that?"

"It's possible, she has a key." Debbie smiles. "But if she was, she never emptied the bins."

***

I'm almost giddy by the time we reach the car. Lillian lied. Innocent people don't lie, they don't need to. It's our first lead, a real lead.

"I can't believe we figured it out. We found the murderer. I mean, I know you said we would, but you say lots of things, so I wasn't expecting... Why are we at a used car showroom?"

Mum unfastens her seatbelt. "This isn't just any used car showroom, it's Paul Marshall's used car showroom."

"What? Why? We solved it. We cleared my name and… Didn't we?"

"Not quite."

"But Lillian lied."

"People lie all the time, it doesn't make them guilty."

I think God would disagree.

"We need more proof, and to rule out the other suspects. Suspects like Karen. You were convinced it was her yesterday."

"That was before Lillian lied. Why else would she lie?"

"Maybe she's covering for someone else, or hiding another secret, or maybe she just didn't feel like working on Monday night."

My enthusiasm ebbs away.

A young man in a hideous hunter-green suit saunters over, a large grin on his face. I can almost read his thoughts. Easy money.

"Ladies, my name's Dave. It'll be my pleasure to assist you today. I have to say, we don't get many sisters coming in here. Are you twins?" His grin widens as vomit rises in my throat. Surely no one falls for that nonsense.

Mum titters, her face reddening. I roll my eyes. Thankfully, Mum's too busy making eyes at Dave to notice.

"If I may ask, which of you lovely young ladies is interested in purchasing one of our fine automobiles today?"

Why are car salesmen always so oily? Is it a prerequisite for the job? Or do they teach them to be that creepy?

"That'd be me," Mum says, averting her gaze.

Dave's a good thirty years younger than her, muscular, with piercing blue eyes, and a mop of auburn curls. He's quite good-looking, once you manage to see past the suit. Which Mum would love to do.

"Well, Miss…" Dave locks eyes with Mum.

"Please, call me Marian."

Please, don't.

"Well, Marian, what kind of car are you looking for?"

"Something red and sporty."

I hope she's still referring to the cars. Please, be referring to the cars.

"But I'll settle for a car." Mum laughs, hitting Dave playfully on the chest.

"Gosh, what a lot of muscles you have, Dave."

Gosh, what a lot of counselling I'm going to need after this.

Mum slips her hand through the crook of Dave's arm as he leads her around the car lot, explaining how wonderful their cars are, especially those costing more than twenty thousand pounds.

He opens the door of one of the cars and stands aside. It's not sporty. It's not even red. What it is, is screaming middle-aged frump.

Howking up her skirt, Mum brushes past Dave and squeezes in. With practised fake gallantry, Dave steps forward and pulls a lever. The seat drops back taking Mum with it. She squawks. Her leg batters the steering column.

Dave turns beetroot. "Oh, I'm sorry, I'm sorry. Wrong lever." He attempts to straighten Mum's clothes.

She slaps him away. "Oi! The least you could do is buy me dinner first."

Dave regains his composure. "Surely a fine creature like yourself already has a man."

Mum adjusts the seat and brings herself upright. "I have many, but there's always room for one more." She and Dave share a salacious grin.

"A woman after my own heart."

"Oh Dave, so naïve. It's not your heart I'm after."

They snigger. I pop open the car's glove box on the off chance there's a sick bag hidden inside. No luck.

Climbing out, Mum rubs a hand over the car's bodywork. "No, this isn't the one. What about that one?"

She points to a car in pride-of-place at the front of the lot.

"That one?" Dave frowns. "Isn't it a little… It's fast right enough. But it's lower than this one, harder too… And it's less roomy…"

"Roomy?" Mum smirks. "Why Dave, what do you think I'll be getting up to in there?"

I interject. Honestly, I'm amazed it's taken me this long. "He means you won't get much in the boot. So it's no good for your life drawing canvases."

"Exactly, it… Life drawing? Isn't that… With the…" He gestures in the general direction of his chest.

Mum grins. "I'm posing for the class tomorrow night if you fancy coming along."

Dave reddens. "Well, I…"

"We're always looking for new models if you'd rather." She steps closer.

Dave steps back. "I… I…"

"How about a test drive?" Mum strokes the car's bonnet.

"I… What? I'm not— Oh, the car. Yes, yes. I'll need a copy of your licence and insurance information." Dave guides us into the showroom and towards a small white desk. To the left, there is a glass-fronted office with a large mahogany desk visible inside.

Mum looks at Dave's little desk in disgust. "Not very big is it?"

He laughs. "It's not the size that matters."

"You're right, Dave, power's important too." She flicks something invisible off the seat in front of Dave's desk. "Unfortunately, you don't seem to have either."

"I… I'm sorry?"

What is she doing?

"Is there a manager I can speak to? I mean, I *am* spending a lot of money." She perches on the edge of the chair.

Dave gives some 'um's, and 'erm's before composing himself. "I'm sorry, Mr Marshall isn't here right now."

Mum sighs dramatically. "When will he be here?"

"I'm not sure."

"Surely you have access to his diary."

"I… Marian, I can assure you, I am more than capable of—"

"It's Miss James."

"I… Yes, of course."

Mum sits in silence, staring at him. Dave hovers over her, seeming unsure of what to do, or say next. Finally, Mum speaks. "The diary, Dave."

"Oh, yes, yes of course." He scurries away, almost bowing as he leaves. I do my best to remain stone-faced.

Within seconds, Dave's back with a tatty brown book. Sighing loudly, Mum snatches it from him and licks her thumb and forefinger before flicking through the pages. I lean over her shoulder.

The diary shows Paul Marshall's full week. Mum taps Monday. Other than a meeting at four PM, the day is blank. She turns the page. The same meeting is scheduled for next Monday too.

"Monday evenings are good for me," Mum says. "When does this meeting usually finish?"

"About five." Dave shifts from foot to foot, unsure how to handle the situation.

"And when do you close?"

"Eight."

"Does Mr Marshall stay until closing?"

"No, he normally heads straight after the meeting. But, I'm sure if I asked—"

"Where does he usually go after leaving here?"

"Well, I… Why are you asking… Who are you?"

Time to go.

Before Dave can have us escorted from the building, I take the diary from Mum and flick back to the previous page. Under Tuesday, scrawled in blue ink are the words: 'Take Mother to the hospital.'

"Right…" Dave snatches up the landline phone and

begins to dial. Mum depresses the button, aiming her...
Well, her assets in Dave's direction.

"Thanks, Dave." She bats her eyelids, all sweetness and
light once more. "Maybe I'll see you tomorrow night at
Life Drawing." With a wink, she turns away and we head
for the door before Dave remembers who he was phoning.

***

It's gone four when we park at the shopping centre and
head to the cinema, with Mum muttering under her breath
about our having to nip home to walk Archibald.

We might not have gotten anywhere finding out Paul
Marshall's whereabouts on Monday night, but maybe we'll
do better confirming Ryan's. This change to the original
plan came after much persuading from me, and much
grumbling from Mum. Not that I think Ryan killed
anyone, but if we're going to do this, we're as well doing it
right.

A young, spotty girl stands at the ticket counter. "Hi,
can I help you?"

Mum leans on the counter. "I hope so. We're private
investigators."

"You're what?"

Yes, we're what?

"Private investigators." Mum repeats.

The girl looks sceptical. I don't blame her, so am I.

Mum takes a rectangular card from her purse and lays it
down.

Marian James
Private Investigator

When did she have those made? And why?

The girl stares at the card. "Do you want the manager?"

"No, we want to speak to anyone who was working on
Monday night."

117

"I'll need to get the manager." The girl heads into a back room.

Mum helps herself to some popcorn. I slap it out of her hand. She sticks her tongue out at me in response.

"I was only going to have a wee taste. It's allowed. Like grapes at the supermarket."

And bottom wipers, and wheelchairs. Apparently.

The manager turns out to be another spotty youth. He looks about fifteen, although, he must be older. Still, at least it'll stop Mum flirting, I've seen enough of that today.

"Can I help you?" The manager asks.

"Why, yes, you can." Mum leans forward, one hand on the counter, the other idly running over the gold chain around her neck.

Not again.

The manager looks genuinely horrified. "S— Sorry?

Slapping the counter in defeat, she draws back and taps her fake business card. "We need to speak to anyone who was working on Monday night."

"I was here, can I help?"

"Actually, yes. I need access to your security recordings." She turns, nodding pleasantries to the customers queuing behind.

The manager hesitates. "Don't you need a warrant or something?"

Oh, we need a lot more than that.

Mum scoffs. "Of course not. Don't they teach you anything?"

"I'm sorry, I don't think—"

"We're investigating a murder," Mum says, her voice loud, assertive. "We believe the main suspect was here on Monday night. He may be planning to use the darkness of your screenings to take another life."

The manager's eyes widen.

"Murder. She said murder." The growing queue share excited whispers, a few hurry for the door.

The manager ushers us through the door behind the

tills. It leads to a flight of stairs at the top of which is a room filled with monitors. A balding man sits watching the screens. He ignores our intrusion. I get the feeling he's in this job for the free popcorn more than anything else.

"What timeframe do you need?" The manager leans over a vacant keyboard.

Mum consults her notebook. It's blank. I wish I could say I was surprised.

"Five PM onwards."

With a few keystrokes, one of the monitors changes to show a crowded lobby.

"Can you speed this up?"

The manager complies and people begin running through the door.

"Faster."

The people shoot across the screen in a manic blur.

Mum giggles. I discreetly elbow her. She sighs. "Fine, slow it down a bit." She peers at the screen. "Stop."

The picture freezes.

"There." She points.

The screen shows Ryan looking up at an older man, something like adoration in his eyes.

"Oh, my god." The manager's hand shoots up to cover his mouth. "Ryan Ritchie's a killer. He lives on my street." He trembles, his eyes wide. "He's just a kid."

Mum looks highly amused. I shake my head and make eyes in the direction of the poor lad. She frowns, and mouths: "What?"

I gesture again, my movements more animated. We stand, swapping hand gestures in a silent argument. By the time Mum concedes, the boy is pacing.

"Don't be daft, whatever made you think Ryan was a killer?"

"But, you said… You said…"

She waves away the words. "I said we were verifying alibis, nothing more."

"You said he might be planning to kill someone in the

cinema. In the dark."

"Nonsense, you must have misheard me."

The boy continues to tremble. Mum pats his arm. "Come on, there's nothing to worry about. Ryan's no murderer, he's not even a suspect."

"But you said…"

She assists the manager onto a chair. "We're looking into a crime, that's right. But Ryan's no suspect. We're just being thorough, ticking people off a list, nothing more."

The manager nods. "Right, right. But, I'm sure you said—"

"I think you've been watching too many horror films." With a mock-sympathetic smile, she continues. "What time did Ryan enter the cinema?"

He points a shaky finger at the bottom of the screen. "Six-fifteen."

"And what time does he leave?"

Reluctantly, he taps in a command. The monitor fast-forwards, then slows to normal speed. The video shows Ryan exiting the lobby at ten to nine. I sigh. He was here, but it doesn't rule him out.

"Thanks…" Mum peers at his name tag. "Dicky."

"It's Ricky."

She shrugs. "If you say so. Now, how about a couple of free tickets to the new Ryan Reynolds film?"

The manager shakes his head. "How about one adult and one child ticket?"

"Throw in a large popcorn and you've got yourself a deal."

"Only if you promise you won't come back."

"We promise we won't come back…" Mum lowers her voice "…Tonight."

CHAPTER SIXTEEN

The next morning, Mum has her MOO board propped up on the kitchen table. I'm tempted to change it to something else while she's out of the room. MOOB board perhaps, that seems quite in keeping with Mum's sense of humour. However, I manage to behave myself, and instead, eat my cereal while Archibald and I watch the kitchen telly.

Maybe being home isn't so bad after all. It's a bit like being a kid again. I'm skint, and my Mum appears every so often with random suggestions before wandering off again. Admittedly, now she isn't followed by an array of strange-looking men, and the stench of alcohol. Well, she doesn't reek of alcohol, at least.

"Nora, are you listening?"

I pull my gaze from the TV. "Sorry, what were you saying?" I didn't hear her come in, let alone hear her speak.

With a sigh, Mum taps the board. "I said we need to tidy this up."

"I can rewrite it if you like." It would help if it was even remotely legible.

Her eyes narrow. "I was thinking more of cutting down the suspects."

I'm confused. I thought that's what we'd been trying to do — very unsuccessfully — for the last few days. I mean, we didn't don wigs and invade a sheltered housing complex just for the fun of it. Well, maybe Mum did.

"Right…" It's the best I can manage.

"So, I vote we go straight to the main suspect, and either convict them or clear them."

"The main suspect other than myself."

"Naturally."

"Because, by the looks of your board, I still look very guilty."

She sighs again. "We've been through this."

"I know, I know. To stay ahead of the police. All I'm saying is maybe don't show your board to PC Fergusson."

"Get dressed, we leave in ten."

"Make it twenty, I need to feed Archibald."

Mum scowls. "When are you getting rid of that… thing?"

"We're not." I rise. "And his name's Archie."

"What happened to his 'bald'? Did you decide it was too ironic?"

I stick my tongue out at her. Picking up my bowl, I carry it to my room, spooning the remaining cereal into my mouth as I go. Mum shouts after me. "Wear something nice."

Define 'nice'. To me, this means something smart, and understated. To Mum, on the other hand…

Twenty minutes later, we're locking the front door and heading for the car. I was right about our definitions of 'nice' varying. Mum didn't half give me an odd look when I came downstairs. Although, my look can't have been much better. I doubt many people can pull off cherry hair, a purple cardigan, and a green dress. And if they can pull it off, they should do so immediately, and burn it. Still, at least it's not a curtain.

I fasten my seatbelt. "To the car lot, Sherlock."

Mum turns off the engine.

"Barnaby?" I suggest.

"Holmes."

"Sorry?"

"It'd be Holmes, not Sherlock."

It takes every bit of my self-control not to roll my eyes. "Does it matter?"

"Not really."

"So…"

"Why the car lot?"

"What?"

"Why the car lot?"

"Because you said—"

"I said we were going to see the main suspect." She says the words slowly, deliberately.

"Right, and that's Paul Marshall."

"Wrong."

"But you said…" I give up. "So, where *are* we going?"

Mum taps the side of her nose and restarts the engine.

When she pulls into an all-too-familiar car park my stomach twists in knots. I'm not ready to be back here.

"Are you coming?" She stands beside the open car door.

You can do this, Nora.

Taking a deep breath, I unclip my seatbelt and follow Mum into the offices of Moorbank Recruitment Consultancy, my head bowed.

Karen is speaking with an elegant older lady in a tweed skirt and jacket when we enter.

"Those aren't skills." Karen sneers.

"I can assure you, shorthand—"

"Is like speaking Latin, or knowing how to sew." Karen leans back in her chair and picks up her mobile.

"Those are very useful skills."

Her finger flicks up the screen.

"Miss Brown?"

Karen ignores her. She's good at that. Perhaps that's one of those 'skills' she keeps talking about.

Tutting, the lady shows herself out. Mum and I take her place. Mum raps on the desk. "Oi, get off your phone."

Karen sighs dramatically. Mum snatches the mobile from her hand.

"Hey—"

Mum taps and swipes.

Karen jumps to her feet. "What are you—"

"Who's Bill?"

"What? No-one. Give me that." Karen makes a grab for the mobile.

Mum dodges her hand. "Looks like a definite someone to me. So does this one, and this one. How many men have you got in here?" Mum turns the phone, her eyebrows rising. "Remind me to ask for a new one of these for Christmas, one with more pixels, or whatever they use these days." She shows me the screen.

"Oh!" I turn away, my face flushing. That was a little more explicit than I was expecting.

Karen makes another lunge for the phone. Mum moves it out of her reach. "If you want it, I suggest you start talking."

Karen growls, and pulls back, stomping her foot.

"Sit."

She sits, her arms crossed.

"Now, stop treating us like we farted at your grandma's funeral, and start answering our questions."

I almost want to stand up and applaud but I think it might give the wrong impression.

Karen growls again. "What?"

"Nora…" Mum turns to me, expectantly.

I wasn't prepared for that. I open my mouth, hoping she'll interrupt and save me. No such luck. "Where…" My voice comes out as a quiet croak, I clear my throat.

You've got this, Nora. "Where were you on Monday night between nine and midnight?"

"It's not her," Mum says with a sigh.

I frown. "What?"

Even Karen looks confused. Mum hands me the mobile. "Her location's on. She was in Edinburgh."

"That only proves that her phone—"

"Look at the pictures."

I hesitate. Given what I saw earlier…

Chuckling, Mum locates the relevant picture and hands the mobile back to me before taking her own phone from her bag.

The screen shows Karen pouting in front of The Dome, the time stamp shows it was taken on Monday at half-eight at night.

"That doesn't mean—"

"Keep scrolling," Mum says, without looking up.

I comply. Karen pouting over a cocktail. Karen posing with a group of friends in a fancy restaurant. Karen and co. flashing their legs to hail a taxi. I check the time. Four in the morning. Mum's right, there's no way Karen could have killed her grandmother.

Karen gives a slow clap. I toss the phone down on her desk, hoping I 'accidentally' crack the screen.

"Pathetic. Like I'd kill my grandma for a lousy one hundred and seventy thousand, five hundred and nine pounds."

Well, that's oddly specific. "And a house." I point out.

Karen scoffs. "Have you seen Daddy's house? Owning a place like that is a total embarrassment." She looks closely at Mum and me for the first time, before continuing. "I liked her, like really liked her. She was always nice to me."

She's lying, she has to be. I can't imagine Mrs Marshall being nice to anyone, not even her own family.

"She taught me how to use people to get what I want. Money, designer clothes…"

Ah, that makes more sense.

"I don't need to kill people to get what I want." She points to her phone. "Bill just bought me a flat near Princes Street."

125

"Is he married?" Mum asks.

Karen shrugs. "Sure, but I like that, makes him more likely to buy me things."

"Shame it'll stop when I tell his wife."

Karen scoffs. "As if."

"I thought your boy Bill looked familiar." Mum turns her mobile around. The screen shows a young muscular man standing next to a pretty woman in a red dress.

"A quick search and there he is with his wife. The caption even gives both their names. From there it was easy to locate this…" She clicks the browser forward to the website of a large charity. Bill's wife beams back at us from the screen. "It won't take me long to get her itinerary." Mum looks smug.

Karen tosses her mobile into her desk drawer. "Tell her. Like she'll believe…" She waggles her finger up and down in the general direction of Mum and her colourful ensemble.

Mum straightens her cardigan. "I'm sure she'll believe the photos I sent from your phone to mine."

Karen looks scared for the first time. "You wouldn't. He's not given me the deeds yet."

Mum feigns sadness. "Aww, I guess you'll be answering the rest of Nora's questions then. And if you do, I'll forget all about tracking down lover boy's better half. Deal?"

Karen rolls her eyes.

"You'll go blind doing that," Mum says, smiling.

Reluctantly, Karen concedes. "Deal."

They look at me expectantly.

Questions? What questions? I thought we'd just eliminated her.

I open my mouth but nothing happens. Mum leans towards me. "Her dad."

"Her dad! I mean, your dad. Where was he on Monday night?"

Karen shrugs.

"Oh, erm… What about the gambling?"

She sighs. "So, he gambles. Lots of men do. It's not a problem, Daddy always makes sure I get whatever I want."

I'm starting to understand why Karen acts the way she does.

"So he doesn't have any money problems?"

She laughs. "You're way off. He just bought a villa in the south of France."

Mum and I exchange glances. Something isn't adding up. Sammy was adamant that Paul Marshall had asked his mother for money. And Paul himself seemed worried that someone called Denny had sent us to pay him a visit.

"Is there anything else? Or can I get back to work?" Karen smirks. "You know, work, that thing you lasted about an hour doing."

To hell with their deal. First chance I get I'm showing those pictures to Bill's wife. That'll wipe that smug smile off her stupid face.

"I'm not finished." Why did I say that?

They wait, Karen looking less than patient, Mum looking confused.

I snatch up a pen and pad of paper from the desk and position them in front of her. "I want a list of everyone your grandmother was blackmailing and what she had on them."

"How would I—"

"As you said, she taught you to use people to get what you want. And I bet her lessons included information on her victims. So start writing or Mum will have those photos sent faster than you can say Carolina Herrera."

***

I did it. I actually did it.

Mum and I sit at her kitchen table staring at the list of names lying before us. Mum slurps her tea. "How did you know Mrs Marshall had told her all that stuff?"

I laugh. "I didn't."

"You were bluffing?"

I think I see a hint of pride in her eyes. Just a hint. "You can't be that surprised. You taught me to play poker." And three-card Monte, and to count cards. Well, she tried, but I was never very good at it. Although, it did make for a rather memorable eighth birthday. Not as memorable as my ninth birthday right enough, when Mum passed out legs akimbo, sprawled on a lawn chair, wearing a tartan miniskirt and no underwear. She'd said it'd be culturally inappropriate to wear underwear. It certainly made her popular with my classmates' dads, their mothers on the other hand…

Mum scores out Karen Brown's name on her MOO board. "All right then, Poirot, who's next?"

I blink. Poirot? I'm the boss? I sip my tea, hiding my smile. "I think we need to start going through the list Karen gave us. Do you recognise any of the names?"

Mum leans over my shoulder. "That one. He's Mrs McGinty's next-door neighbour. I'll call her now and see if she knows where he was on Monday." Picking up the list, Mum heads to the living room.

Smiling, I stretch my legs out on the chair opposite. Archie makes a jump for my lap, his front paws landing on my thighs before he falls back down. I scoop him up, ruffling his fur. "Come on, let's take you for a walk."

Clicking on his lead, we head over the road and down into the valley. The bushes flanking the path are still damp from the rain overnight. At the bottom of the hill, I turn left. A group of children chase each other around the park, kicking woodchips into the air.

On a nearby bench, watching the kids, sits Lillian Grant. She has an open book in her hand, but her eyes are fixed on a little boy with dark hair and freckles.

Tugging Archie's lead, I direct him towards the bench. Lillian lowers her eyes and stares at her book, ignoring me as I sit down.

"Hello again."

She moves along the bench.

"Is that your son?"

She drops the book into her handbag and makes to stand. As if sensing the movement, the little boy runs over.

"Why did you lie, Lillian?"

The boy looks from his mother to me. He buries his head in her coat.

"The police know you lied." Now who's lying? But the bluff pays off.

"Go play, baby. Mummy's just talking to this woman." With a reassuring smile, she nudges him towards his friends. The boy looks uncertain as he retreats to watch from a safe distance. Lillian feigns a laugh and waves. I don't think she's fooling anyone.

"What do you want?" Her voice is low, angry.

"The truth."

"I told you the truth."

"No, you said you cleaned Hall-In Care on Monday night, but Debbie waited for you, and you never showed."

Lillian giggles nervously. "I must have got muddled up. An honest mistake."

"No, Lillian, it wasn't. Where were you on Monday night?"

She lowers her head. "I didn't do it."

"Do what?"

"Any of it. The stuff that old… What does it matter now?"

I nod towards her son. "It'll matter to him if PC Fergusson drags you down the station for questioning. That won't be so easy to explain away."

She picks at her nails. "I can't lose him. I won't…"

"Then talk to me, I can help."

Lillian's laugh is almost hysterical. "You! What can you do? What can anyone do?"

"I can expose Mrs Marshall for what she was."

"What good is that now?"

"It'd explain why you—"

"Why I what? Killed her? I didn't kill her, I couldn't have. I was—" Lillian shakes her head and hurries towards her son. Taking his hand, she rushes down the path away from the park.

Mrs Marshall had something on Lillian, something big.

CHAPTER SEVENTEEN

There's fresh tea and biscuits on the table when Archie and I return. My stomach tightens. "What happened?"

"Who says anything's happened?"

I nod towards the plate. Chocolate Digestives. "You've got the bad news biscuits out."

Mum sighs. "Fine. I spoke to Mrs McGinty. The list Karen gave you is fake."

"What? All of it."

"All of it. So, either her precious grandma fed her a pack of lies or…"

"Or Karen made it up."

She nods.

"Are you sure? There must be fifteen names on there."

"Real names, false information." Mum places the list on the table. "See that woman there, she did have an affair but not with that man. It was years ago, I remember it. More importantly, her husband knows about it too. They worked things out and stayed together. Then this man here, he didn't kill his wife, he couldn't have. He has an alibi."

"What alibi?"

"Erm… Well, let's just say I can vouch for him."

My eyes narrow. "I thought you didn't sleep with married men."

She harrumphs. "Who said anything about sleeping with him? We were playing darts down at The Moorpond if you must know."

"Then why not say that?"

Mum grins sheepishly. "Well, it was a little after hours… About three in the morning."

"So?"

"And Freddie didn't exactly give us access. The window latch in the ladies' lavvy was loose."

Of course it was.

"Or it was, once Alf had given it a persuasive nudge."

I stare at the list. "All of them?"

Mum holds up the plate of biscuits. "Chocolate Digestive?"

I take one and dunk it idly in my tea. She lied. Why does everyone keep lying to us?

"Nora…"

I dunk the biscuit over and over. Why not just tell us the truth?

"Nora…"

I mean, know Karen's a b—

"Nora!" Mum dabs the puddle of tea surrounding my mug with a paper napkin. Half my biscuit is missing, no doubt lurking somewhere at the bottom of the cup. I toss the remaining Chocolate Digestive in to join it. Bad news biscuits indeed.

Mum clears away the dishes. "What's that?"

"What?"

"On the floor, what's… That fluffy ferret has shredded a stick all over the lino. Where did you take him? Through the woods?"

I shake my head. "The park, and guess who we bumped into."

"Thora Hurd." She says, deadpan.

"What? Why would she be at the park?"

"With her great-grandkids."

"In Moorbank?"

She shrugs.

I frown. "Isn't she dead?"

Another shrug. "Everyone's dead these days."

I'm not sure how to answer that, so instead, I fill her in on my conversation with Lillian.

"That one's got secrets even *she* doesn't know about."

Is that possible? I decide against asking. "She definitely knows more than she's letting on."

Mum gestures at my clothes with her half-eaten biscuit. "She bribable?"

"I doubt it. Her son might be."

"That could work. I'll get the chocolate."

I laugh. "That's all we need, you down the play park offering kids sweets." I shake my head. "I think we should move on." Taking the whiteboard marker, I point at the board. "And I vote for Barbara Veitch. She's easier to track down than the others and can give us background on both Jamesina Marshall and Paul Marshall."

Mum grins. "You're starting to think like a real detective."

I smile, tossing the marker back on the table. Maybe if my plan to retrain as an occupational therapist doesn't work out, I could join the police. I couldn't do any worse than PC Fergusson.

"But you've missed something."

Then again… I frown at the board but no matter how much I scowl, nothing comes to mind.

"She was probably there on Monday…" Mum prompts.

Still nothing.

"She might have seen something suspicious…"

Realisation sets in. "Or *someone* suspicious."

Mum claps her hands together. "I'll get my keys."

Grabbing my bag, I give Archie a farewell kiss on the head and follow Mum to the car.

***

Calburn Court's car park is almost empty when we pull in. I scan the cars as if I might recognise one of them. I don't.

Ms Veitch's office door is ajar when we arrive. Through the gap, I spot her at her desk writing something on a pad of paper. Why couldn't she have been having an incriminating phone conversation? Or be disposing of evidence? That's always the way it is on TV.

"Anything interesting going on in there?" Mum pushes me aside. "She's alone, how boring. Hang on, where—"

The door is thrown open. We step back, straightening up.

"Ms Beitch, so lovely to see you again." Mum offers a grin.

Veitch glares at us. "Spying again. Don't you two have anything better to do?"

"Actually, no." Mum pushes past her and plonks herself down in Veitch's swivel chair. "So, since we're all here, let's have a chat."

"A chat? How civilised." Veitch crosses her arms. "I would have thought sneaking around in ridiculous budget Halloween wigs and breaking into apartments was far more your style."

Sounds like Karen Brown's been filling her in on our run-in at Mrs Marshall's place. Just how friendly are they? Does she know about Ms Veitch and her dad?

"Who's Terry?" Mum glances over the papers on Veitch's desk.

"What?" Veitch asks with an exasperated sigh.

Mum speaks slowly, raising her voice. "Terry. Who is he?"

"Why?"

She shrugs. "Humour me."

Veitch stares at the wall briefly before her gaze returns

to Mum. "My aerobics instructor. Anything else?"

"Yes, were you two…" Mum waggles her eyebrows.

"Does that matter?"

Mum giggles. "Poor Pauly. Finding out from his mother like that. Must have made you pretty angry."

Veitch scoffs. "Angry enough to kill? Sorry to burst your bubble, Columbo, but I didn't know he knew. Not until after…" She adjusts her stance.

Sadly, she's telling the truth. Mum and I overheard that conversation the last time we eavesdropped at her office door.

"Does Terry have room for a new client?" Mum sounds hopeful. "I enjoy a good squat."

I clear my throat loudly.

"Fine, fine." She sighs and leans back in the chair. "Where were you on Monday night?"

"Pass." Veitch glares in my direction. "Shouldn't it be good cop's turn? I'm assuming that's why she's here. Or did you just need a human stutter machine for ambience?" She looks me up and down. I've never seen anyone look so offended by a simple jeans and jumper combo. I say simple, my jeans are designer, and my jumper — a present from Emma — is from Harvey Nics.

"I—"

Mum cuts me off. "Never mind her. Back to Monday night."

"You can ask as many times as you like. I'm not going to answer."

Mum harrumphs. "Fine. What about the daily cleaning? And having control over the café menu?"

"Mrs Marshall paid for additional privileges. Any of our other clients are welcome to do the same."

"So, she wasn't blackmailing you?"

"No."

"And you have records of the payments she made for these extra services?"

Veitch almost growls her response. "Yes, and I can

produce them if I have to. For someone with the right to ask and a warrant."

Mum nods slowly. "How did she feel about you sleeping with her son?"

Veitch's jaw flexes. Mum's eyes narrow. "I take it she wasn't pleased."

"Paul's a grown man. He can do what he likes."

"Or who he likes," Mum adds with a chuckle. "What about his wife?"

There's a beat before she answers. "They're separated."

"Were they separated before you two started doing the no-trouser tango?"

I close my eyes. No matter how old you are, you should never have to hear your own mother using euphemisms for... well, that.

"What business is it of yours?"

Mum shrugs. "I'm nosy."

"That's not my problem."

"It is if you want us to leave without making a fuss." Mum crosses her arms. "I can scream rather loudly if I have to. And you already know I can act."

If you can call making lewd remarks while wearing a curtain, acting.

Veitch sighs heavily. "They were having... issues. Practically divorced. Anyway, it's all out in the open now, so what does it matter?"

"So, his wife and daughter know it was you he was having an affair with?"

"They don't need to know."

That'd be a 'no' then.

Mum continues. "We went to see Paul yesterday, at the car lot, but he wasn't there."

"Lucky him."

"Do you know where else we might find him?"

Veitch rolls her eyes. "Do I look like his keeper?"

"A strong woman like you, I bet that's exactly what you are. I bet you tell him what to do, and he does it, tail wagging."

Veitch looks Mum up and down as if re-appraising her. "Rybrookes, most likely. The bookies down the centre."

"What was Mrs Marshall like?"

"Your silent partner met her. She knows."

Mum answers before I have the chance to defend myself. "She met her once, you knew her better."

Veitch unfolds her arms, seeming to relax a little. "What do you want to know? She was a client, nothing more."

"But she was more demanding than most."

She snorts. "You're joking. Half the residents think reaching eighty somehow gives them the right to act a certain way. You should come here at dinnertime. It can be quite eye-opening. Room Nine's deaf, she just…" She gestures low, a look of disgust on her face.

"Pees everywhere?" Mum offers.

"What? No." Veitch looks horrified. "If they're… like that, we insist on pads or catheters. All our seat pads are hand-sewn, hand-wash only. Even the slightest stain…" She shakes her head, the idea seeming to unnerve her.

Mum pulls the cushion out from behind her back and inspects the stitching. She doesn't look impressed. "What then?"

"She… Breaks wind. Freely." Veitch wrinkles her nose. "She can be rather loud, and pungent. She doesn't even try to hide it. This is an upmarket complex, we don't expect…"

"People dropping air biscuits?" Suggests Mum.

I chuckle.

"Quite." Veitch looks less than amused.

"Rather harsh don't you think, I mean if you need to squeeze cheese, there's not much you can do about it. Well, maybe a funny walk, but that would just be silly."

Says the woman who sprinted down the corridor cupping her bosoms.

Veitch glares at her. "Finished?"

Mum laughs. "Oh, come on Veitch, what's the harm in a wee one-cheek squeak, well, not unless…" Her eyes widen. "She didn't?" Her lips purse as she tries to suppress a smile. "Did she follow through?"

Veitch growls and points to the door. "Out."

Mum rocks back, chuckling. "Was it on your exclusive fabby-dabby hand-sewn seat pads? She clutches her stomach, laughing uncontrollably. "Oh!" Her face pales. She sits up, clutching herself.

My jaw drops. She didn't… Did she?

Veitch reddens. "Get. Out."

Blushing, Mum straightens. "Where were you on Monday night?"

"You just—"

"Lovely cushions you have, it'd be a shame if you couldn't attend to them quickly." Mum shifts from side to side.

Veitch's jaw clenches. I swear I hear her teeth grinding.

"I was here. Obviously."

"Until when?"

"Eight sharp."

"That's very precise."

"I have a strict schedule." Veitch eyes the cushion under Mum's bum.

"Where did you go after?"

"To the gym. I had spin class from eight-thirty until nine-thirty, then I showered and left the gym at ten."

Another suspect with precise responses. Unfortunately, I believe her.

"Did you see anything suspicious before you left here?" Mum asks.

"Like two old women running about in wigs?"

Did she just call me old?

Mum scoffs. "That was Wednesday, I asked about Monday."

"Someone running out of Mrs Marshall's covered in cake, perhaps? No, nothing, and no one."

"Where did you go after the gym?" Mum crosses her legs. It's a bit late now.

"Home." Growls Veitch.

"Can anyone vouch for you?"

"A troupe of half-naked men."

I blink. I must have misheard.

"You might know them." The comment is directed at Mum. Veitch looks like she's up to something, but whether she knows it or not, she's probably right.

I clear my throat which is beginning to feel rather dry and take a sudden interest in the pictures on Veitch's wall. They're abstract with blobs of colour and no discernible pattern. They resemble something Emma might have painted in primary school.

"Is one of them a stripper named Mike?" Mum asks.

A strip… Oh, for heaven's sake.

Veitch raises an eyebrow. "I wouldn't have thought it'd be your kind of entertainment."

"You'd be surprised."

She certainly would. When I was younger, Mum regularly fell through the front door, and pass out on the couch with money sticking out of her skirt and the odd g-string in her hand. I soon got to recognise the stamps of most of the strip clubs in Glasgow. Goodness knows what she got up to, I never dared ask.

"So, no alibi from ten onwards?" Mum idly flicks through the papers on Veitch's desk.

"Correct. Now, get out of my chair." Veitch is almost beetroot now. The colour goes beautifully with her blue skirt suit.

Harrumphing, Mum stands. Veitch steps forward to inspect the damage. Pulling a latex glove from a box, she snaps it on and runs her hand over the stitching.

Mum pats my arm. "Let's leave her to it."

As we close the office door behind us, Mum's stomach rumbles. "Fancy nipping into Mrs Baillie's for some tea and cake?"

"Shouldn't you…" My gaze flicks to her skirt.

She laughs. "I may be old, but I've not lost control of my bladder just yet."

"You…"

She grins. "I told you I could act."

Laughing, we head towards Mrs Baillie's in search of sustenance. After a brief knock, we let ourselves in without awaiting an invitation. I'm already salivating at the thought of all that cake. But no sweet smell greets us, and the living room sits empty.

"She must be out." There goes my chance of cake.

"Or she's fallen," Mum suggests. "We should make sure."

I nod.

Mum takes the bathroom while I chap lightly on the bedroom door and push it open. The bed is neatly made and the curtains are open. On the nightstand sits a framed photo of Mrs Baillie in her youth, standing next to an older gentleman.

Perching on the edge of the bed, I pick up the photograph. The man looks vaguely familiar.

Mum sighs and leans against the bedroom doorway. "It's no good, there's not even cake in the fridge."

So much for searching for Mrs Baillie.

"What's that?"

I show her the picture. "Do you know him?"

"No. Him, I'd remember."

Frowning, I return the picture to its rightful place, and we show ourselves out.

Stomachs rumbling, we drive to the local shopping centre to grab some lunch, purposely passing Rybrookes on the way.

The shop smells of sweat. There are three men propped up at a narrow counter on the left, and another on a stool, yelling at the wall-mounted TV. It sounds like he's about to win big.

I scan the room. In the far corner sits the hunched

figure of Paul Marshall.

Walking over, Mum sits herself down on the stool next to him. "Christian."

He stares at her, a look of confusion on his face before recognition sets in and his eyes narrow. "What do *you* want?"

"Answers." Mum's smile widens. She almost looks innocent.

Paul screws up his betting slip and tosses it on the floor. I pick it up and glance around for a bin. Not finding one, I slip it into the pocket of my jeans.

"How much?"

His question catches me off guard, but Mum seems prepared. "Twenty bucks for the lot."

He scoffs. "That won't even…" He rubs his hand over his face. "All right, fine."

Mum hands over the money. "Batter up." She steps aside.

I look from her to Paul and back. "What, me?"

"The bases are loaded."

I don't know what that means. I'm not even sure Mum knows what that means.

"Step up to the plate."

I take the smallest step. "Tell us about your mum."

Paul laughs. It's an ugly, hateful laugh. "You're being polite calling her that. She was cruel, demanding, manipulative."

Not close then. "Was she blackmailing you?"

"Me? Why would she? I have nothing to give her."

"Swing and a miss." Mum mimes the action.

I glare at her and continue. "What about Barbara Veitch?"

"Why would she blackmail me?"

I blush. "No, I… Was your mum blackmailing her?"

Paul considers. "It's possible. Barbie has easy access to a good bit of cash."

Did he just call her 'Barbie'? The woman resembles a

Rottweiler.

"Is that a 'yes'?"

He shrugs. "It's an 'I don't know'. You'd need to ask her."

This isn't getting us anywhere. I shake my head, searching for questions, and coming up blank. There must be something. I close my eyes, retracing our steps in my mind. Mrs Marshall's accusations, my pathetic plan to find her necklace, only to find… But why did *I* find…

I fix my gaze on Paul. "Why didn't you find your mother's body?"

"What?" He turns back to the TV screen. The horses gallop over the finish line. He groans.

"Your mother," I say, raising my voice. "Why didn't you find her? You were supposed to take her to her hospital appointment. You should have been there before…" Before me. If he had, would I be any less of a suspect than I am now?

Paul runs his hand through the remains of his hair. "I… We argued. The day before."

An old man pushes past, heading to the counter to collect his winnings. Paul glares at him with hatred. Seeming to feel my gaze, he composes himself.

"What about?"

"Money. What else? The old b—" He shakes his head. "She was loaded. I just needed a little to tie me over. Denny was… There were threats. She could have—"

A few patrons roar at the screen, cursing their luck.

"What about your new villa in the south of France."

"My what? Oh, that." He searches his pockets. "I showed Kiki and Barbie some pictures I got online, tried to get them to go halfers. They almost fell for it too." He holds his thumb and forefinger a centimetre apart. "I was this close…"

Kiki? That must be his nickname for Karen. It's cute, shame about the owner. "Have you had the will reading?"

Paul grumbles, rolling his shoulders back. I take that as

a yes. "Who inherited from your Mum's death?"

He screws up his face as if the response tastes bitter on his tongue. "Kiki."

"Did you know you weren't her heir?"

"No." The word is angry, spat out from between clenched teeth.

I step back. "Did your mum tell you that she was going to reinstate you as heir? Because we heard…"

Paul's eyes bore into mine. I open my mouth, but the words fail to form. Taking another step back, I grip Mum's arm and guide her towards the door. As it closes behind us, Mum leans closer. "I'd say that was a home run."

CHAPTER EIGHTEEN

"Why can't we go to the police?" I ask, my voice louder than intended. A few customers turn to stare. Mum glares at them and they soon return to their conversations. Or, at least, they pretend to.

We're sitting in the large seating area of a budget café chain. It's gone one, and the café's almost full. Thankfully, the noise of the other customers drones out our conversation to all but a few.

I repeat the question, my voice just above a whisper.

"With what?" Mum picks the cucumber out of her salad sandwich.

"He thought he was going to inherit, that's a good motive. And he certainly has the means."

"And the opportunity?"

I sigh. "I don't know."

"It's not enough, Nora. PC Fergusson will laugh you out of the station."

"If he doesn't throw you in a cell for interfering in an ongoing police investigation." Mr Pender bites into his pepperoni pizza slice. We bumped into him at the counter, it turns out his office is located on the nearby boulevard.

"Why would anyone reinstate that man as their heir?" I

sip my tea.

"Assuming she planned to." Mr Pender picks a piece of pepperoni from between his teeth. "She could have been lying."

"But why—"

Mum snaps her fingers, interrupting me. "Of course, get Sammy all worked up and worried, bring out his protective side. Next thing he knows, he's waiting at the foot of the aisle for her to wobble her way down."

Seems unlikely. Then again, Mum always did know how to manipulate men.

Mr Pender dabs his mouth with a beige paper napkin and continues. "Fill me in on what you've got so far."

I place my hand on Mum's to silence her. "Wouldn't our telling you make you an accomplice?"

He smiles. "She's a smart one, this girl of yours."

"Naturally," Mum says, grinning.

He shrugs. "So, don't tell me."

Mum pushes her sandwich aside and picks a piece of pepperoni off Mr Pender's pizza before pulling the rest of the slice towards her. "We have not ruled out Karen Brown, Mrs Marshall's niece and heir."

Mr Pender nods.

"And we have not ruled in Paul Marshall, who is not furious about his mum leaving her money to his daughter, and who does not have a gambling problem and debts."

All these negatives are starting to get confusing.

Mr Pender slurps his milkshake. "So, who doesn't that leave?"

"The warden, the cleaner, and the gardener."

"And the potential love interest," I add, much to Mum's annoyance. "And the neighbour."

"I keep telling you, Nora, nobody kills over cake."

"You'd be surprised." Mr Pender rescues his pizza. "However, in this case, the gardener did it."

I frown. "Are you sure?"

He nods sagely. "It's definitely him."

"But Mr Pender—"

"Call me Matty."

I ignore him. "I can't—"

"Hush, Nora." Mum pats my arm. "Let the adults talk."

I glare at her. She does know I'm older than Mr Pender, doesn't she?

"Why are you so sure it's him?" Mum eyes the pizza.

"Well, I certainly don't have an informant at the police station, who did not confirm Ryan Ritchie's alibi."

Oh, for heaven's sake, is everyone speaking in riddles now?

Mr Pender continues through a mouthful of pizza. "Ryan Ritchie's dad didn't admit to staying up half the night with Ryan after the film because there wasn't a storm that night, and Ryan isn't scared of thunder."

What did he say? I look to Mum who simply nods.

Mr Pender stands. "Best get back. Nora, Marian, always good not seeing you." With a wink, he heads back to work.

My confusion must be evident on my face because Mum chuckles and explains. "Ryan's been ruled out."

I nod. Progress. That leaves Barbara Veitch who is strong enough to have committed the murder, but who we can't prove had a motive. Paul Marshall has the means and motive, but we don't know if he had the opportunity. And Lillian Grant who we don't have an alibi or a motive for. But we know she *has* a motive, a secret one we can't prove.

Did I say progress? At this rate, we'll find the murderer in time for my trial.

Mum tilts her head. "Penny for them?"

I sigh. "Nobody's talking and nobody's going to crack. And I'm still looking like a very good suspect."

"They'll crack."

"How? They won't even speak to us."

Mum smiles. "Who says they have to?"

***

Debbie paces her office, tapping a pen against her hand. "You want me to lie?"

Mum shakes her head. "No, we want you to help prove that Nora's innocent."

"By lying?"

"By acting."

Debbie laughs. "Do I look like Olivia Colman?"

Mum considers this. "Well, no. But perhaps if you got a perm…"

I knew this was a bad idea, but, yet again, Mum persuaded me to go along with it. If only she could represent me in court, I'd be home free.

"I don't know if you're trying to flatter me, Miss James—"

"Call me Marian."

"But I'm not that easily persuaded, Marian. Lillian's a good worker. She's done nothing to cause me to mistrust her."

"Other than saying she was here on Monday night when she wasn't," Mum says with a look of pure innocence.

Debbie stops pacing. "She could have been here. She could have been late. She could have just forgotten to empty the bins."

Mum's brow creases. "Did you tell the police she was here?"

"They haven't asked anything about her, only…" Her face flushes.

I finish the sentence. "Only about me."

She sighs. "And it's not just me they've been asking. They've been to every client you visited during your induction, getting statements, asking if anything is missing…"

"Just PC Fergusson?" Mum asks.

"No, there was a DI, too. Buchanan, I think. They came separately, asked lots of the same questions." Debbie

147

perches on the edge of her desk.

"They'll be asking about Lillian soon enough if they're smart." Mum leans forward in her chair, trying to catch Debbie's eye. "Mrs Marshall had something on her. Something worth lying about."

Debbie turns away, staring blankly out of the window.

"Mum's right, Debbie. I spoke to her myself. She practically ran away when I questioned her. She was scared."

"Well, you are the prime suspect." Mum props her legs up on Debbie's desk. Debbie knocks them off.

"Not of me," I growl. "She's in trouble." I look pleadingly at Debbie. "She needs your help, we both do."

Debbie's shoulders slump. "What will you do with the information?"

"Whatever we have to," Mum says.

Debbie shakes her head and resumes pacing. "No, I'm sorry."

I open my mouth to beg her to reconsider, but Mum interrupts before I have the chance. "No problem, Debs." She places her feet back on the desk. "Unless she's guilty, of course." She helps herself to the plate of biscuits. "Then what's to say it'll just be Mrs Marshall who gets killed."

"She's not guilty. She can't be." Debbie stares pointedly at Mum's feet.

Mum shrugs. "If you say so." She bites into a plain Digestive. "Be a shame if you're wrong. Especially, if people were to find out you'd been warned and did nothing…"

The office falls silent as Mum's words sink in. Debbie's eyes glisten. "It can't be her."

"Then she has nothing to worry about." Mum places the plate back down. "And neither do you."

Debbie looks anxious and unsure. As powerful as Mum's words, they haven't had the desired effect.

"Has Lillian seemed different at all recently?" I ask.

Debbie pouts, considering. "Well, she's been a little

distracted. And her cleaning's not been up to her normal standard. Missing the skirting boards, things like that. I asked her about it, but she said her boy was having some issues after her divorce." She shrugs. "It's a plausible excuse."

"So is blackmail," Mum adds.

Debbie groans. "Fine, what do I have to do?"

***

At eight PM on the dot, Mum and I peek through a gap in the bathroom door as Lillian enters Hall-In Care. Debbie stands to greet her. "Thanks for coming in a few days early, Lillian. I swear I don't know how this place gets so messy sometimes."

I do. Mum took great pleasure from punching holes in every scrap bit of paper she could get her hands on, then shaking the little circles — chads, Debbie called them — around the room while singing to Taylor Swift. As well as messing up the office sufficiently to warrant an additional cleaning, it also eased the tension. Debbie even joined in, accompanying me and Mum by clicking staples rhythmically over the floor.

Lillian sets up, pulling an old upright vacuum cleaner from the cupboard. Debbie looks nervous, unsure. She sits at the desk, staring at Lillian.

"She'll give the game away if she doesn't stop that." Mum hisses in my ear.

"Shh!"

"Oh, shush yourself!"

We fall silent and continue to watch. Lillian pauses and looks around at Debbie who averts her eyes and quickly begins typing.

Working in silence, Lillian meticulously polishes and vacuums the outer office. At twenty past, she returns to the cupboard and gathers a mop and bucket before approaching the bathroom.

Mum's grip tightens on my shoulder. I want to run. Lillian's hand reaches for the door handle.

"Lillian, do you have a minute?"

I let out a breath as Lillian turns and sits herself down in the chair proffered by Debbie.

"I hope I'm not over-stepping, Lillian, but… Well, it's your work, it hasn't been quite itself. Well, until tonight." Debbie scowls, seemingly aware of her awkward wording.

Lillian giggles nervously, her face reddens. "I… Sorry, Debbie. It won't happen again."

"Are things getting better with your boy?"

Lillian nods. "Much." She makes to stand.

"Wait!" Debbie glances around as if seeking inspiration.

"Pretend to be psychic." Mum wiggles her fingers in Debbie's direction. "Pretend to be psychic."

I frown. "Really?"

She shrugs. "Not my fault she's not blessed with my gift."

And she can't hear you. And she's not crazy. And neither is Lillian. And you're not psychic!

"I feel…" Debbie intertwines her fingers. "That there's something else." She watches Lillian in silence.

The wall clock ticks. Mum breaks wind, loudly and pungently. Thankfully Lillian doesn't seem to have heard. Either that, or she thinks it was Debbie, and she's too polite to say anything. Mum's shoulders shake.

In the office, Debbie's nose wrinkles. She clears her throat. Lillian looks back at the bathroom. I think we've been rumbled.

"I should get on. Those toilets could do with a good clean." Lillian gets to her feet.

"It's the drains. They've been backing up all week. The plumber's coming tomorrow."

"Still…"

"Lillian, please." Debbie walks round to the other side of the desk. "Look, if it's financial, if you need some extra hours, you're welcome to start coming here twice a week."

Lillian lowers her head. "Thanks, Debbie. I appreciate that. But I think it's all behind me now."

"Now that Jamesina Marshall's dead?"

Lillian gasps. "Debbie, I…"

"I heard rumours… Blackmail. Making people do things they…" Debbie shakes her head. "I don't normally take notice of such things but… A friend told me. I know she can't be alone."

My heart lifts, did Debbie just refer to me as a friend?

Lillian's lip quivers. "She… She said I'd stolen from her, she made me do things. If I'd known she was going to die, I wouldn't have… I didn't see any other way."

Debbie drops to her knees in front of Lillian, clasping her hands. "What did she make you do?"

Lillian sniffs loudly. "I lied. I wasn't here on Monday night, I'm sorry. I wasn't going to charge you for tonight to make up for it."

Debbie squeezes her hands. "I don't care about that. I'm worried about you. Talk to me."

"There's a man at Calburn Court, Ted Burns. She… I had to spend time with him, try to get information. I wasn't going to… I wouldn't have…" Lillian wipes the tears from her face. "Mr Burns was a true gentleman, all he talked about was his wife. He was devoted to her." She smiles, then her face falls. "I was there until morning, going through photos, hearing stories." Lillian licks her lips. "When I left without the information, I was so scared. If I'd known…"

Mum and I step back from the door. Poor Lillian. I got off lightly. It sounds as though Mrs Marshall would have stopped at nothing to get what she wanted.

"There's something else, Debbie. Something awful. Something I'll never forgive myself for."

Mum's eyes widen. Reluctantly, I return to my post by the door.

"I didn't kill her, I wouldn't, I couldn't. I was with Mr Burns anyway, but I did… something."

"Okay…"

"I have to tell someone. It's been haunting me."

"It's okay Lillian, you can tell me."

"Yes Lillian, you can tell her." Mum whispers. "Come on, some of us are late for life drawing."

I roll my eyes. Thankfully, Mum doesn't see me. The last thing I need is another warning about Mrs McGinty's third cousin.

Lillian takes a breath, then continues. "She kept on at me, the accusations, the comments, the demands. And I know she got one of her minions to let down my tyres last month, she all but admitted it. It might not sound like much, but between the cost of the recovery truck and the extra babysitting charges from rescheduling my clients, it practically took me into the red."

"What did you do?"

Lillian sighs. "I… Look, I didn't want her to die or anything…"

"But you did try to hurt her?"

She nods.

"What did you do?"

Lillian's voice is quiet, we strain to hear her response.

"You put what, where?" Debbie asks, frowning.

Lillian takes a deep breath. "I spread soap scum over her bathroom floor."

Soap scum. That explains the strange powdery substance that stuck to my trousers when I was searching for the locket. And why the floor felt worn — the non-slip surface was coated in soap.

Lillian continues, more animated now. "The floor slopes there, at the drain. I was careful, making it thicker further in. Once it hardened, you couldn't really see it." She squeezes Debbie's hands, almost pleadingly. "It wouldn't have killed her. I'd never do that. I just thought if she broke her hip, maybe it'd stop for a bit."

Debbie averts her eyes.

"I'm sorry, Debbie, but your girls would have been

okay. They wear shoes, and they never go that far in. It'd only really be slippery right under the shower, and only when the water was running.

Lillian had put a lot of effort into planning her attack, and it might have worked too if someone else hadn't gotten to Mrs Marshall first.

We wait until Debbie has walked Lillian to her car before coming out of hiding. Mum introduces herself to the staff kitchen and fills the kettle.

Debbie locks the front door. "That poor girl."

"I think it helped, talking, I mean." I offer Debbie a smile.

She smiles back. "I hope so."

CHAPTER NINETEEN

The next morning, Mum has her MOO board out before I enter the kitchen. It sits on a chair staring at me. Lillian Grant's name has been scored out. I don't argue. I don't feel the need to check her alibi any more than Mum does. Neither of us doubts the honesty of her tears.

Mum lays a plate of bacon on the table. "Eat up, big day ahead."

I stare at the grease, my stomach flips. "Thanks, but I'll stick to cereal."

Shrugging, Mum pours the contents of my plate onto hers, grease and all. Archie licks his lips and makes eyes at Mum. She blows on a small bit of bacon before throwing it into the air for him to catch.

I help myself to cereal and slice a banana on top. "We're running out of suspects."

"That's a good thing, means we're closer to finding the murderer."

I survey the board. "So, who's next? Sammy or Mrs Baillie?"

Mum gives me a piteous look. "You don't honestly think it could be either of them, do you? Surely by now, even you've figured out it was Paul Marshall."

Even me? What does she mean 'even me'? "We need to be sure. PC Fergusson would be only too happy to lock me up. We can't leave any room for doubt."

"Really, Nora. What would Mrs Baillie's motive be? And don't say cake."

I was going to say cake, people can get very protective of family recipes. "Maybe she wasn't as pleased about dog excrement as she said." I stroke Archie's fur.

"Fine, but she didn't do anything to Sammy. Why's he on the board?"

"You were the one who suggested we add him."

"Yes, and discount him."

I sigh. "Why did you add him then?"

She shrugs. "He's an anomaly. Someone Mrs Marshall was nice to."

She's right, nobody had anything nice to say about Mrs Marshall, not even her son. Well, except Karen, but only if you stretch the definition of the word 'nice'.

"I think we should talk to Sammy again," I say with a decisive nod.

Dressing quickly, I hurry downstairs, searching for my bag. In the car, perhaps? With a sigh, I unlock the front door. PC Fergusson stands on the doorstep. "Going somewhere, Mrs McIntyre?"

This can't be good. He steps into the house, forcing me back.

Archie barks, bounding up and down as Fergusson swings the front door closed. "You weren't thinking of doing a runner now, were you?"

Mum appears at the top of the stairs. "She has no reason to run."

No, but I do have a very good reason for not wanting you in this house. Please tell me Mum's hidden the MOO Board.

I gesture towards the door. "We were on our way to—"

"To the airport?" Fergusson suggests.

"To the supermarket," Mum says, pulling a personal shopping trolley out from the upstairs cupboard and bumping it down the steps into the living room.

Where on earth did she get that thing — other than from the upstairs cupboard — and why? She'd never use something like that and she certainly doesn't need it. It must be for some ruse or another. Either that or it was up for grabs in a skip somewhere. I can imagine her, feet up in the air, skirt up around her waist, stuck in a skip trying to reach the things she thought she could sell.

"We're out of sanitary towels." Mum's comment has the desired effect.

PC Fergusson pales. "Ah, well. This won't take long." He heads for the kitchen. I mouth to Mum about the MOO board.

"What?"

"The board." I hiss.

Mum winks and follows Fergusson into the kitchen. He's standing by the table, a look of disgust on his face. The dishes are piled in the sink, and the work surfaces are covered with assorted junk mail and coupons, but it's hardly filthy.

He scowls at a chair and then seems to think better of it. "It's been brought to my attention that you two have been interfering in an ongoing police investigation."

Uh, oh. I look at Mum, unsure how to answer.

"And which investigation would that be?" She asks, innocently.

PC Fergusson's eyes narrow. Mum offers him a biscuit which he declines. Admittedly, I would have too, it's a dog biscuit. She offered him a bone-shaped, meat-flavoured dog biscuit.

Mum tosses the treat to Archie. "You'll have to be more specific."

"Will I?" And why's that?"

Mum frowns. "Because we have no idea what you're talking about."

"Really? So, you're unaware that your daughter is a suspect in an ongoing murder investigation? The chief suspect, nonetheless."

"Is she? I thought that was all done and dusted, didn't you, Nora?"

"I… I…" I have no idea what to say.

Fergusson scoffs. "Did you really? And why is that?"

She shrugs. "Well, Nora's here, and we've not heard from you in, what… Well, since you tried to assault our solicitor."

The policeman's ears redden. I may not have known what to say, but I certainly wouldn't have said that.

"I can assure you, Miss James, Nora remains very much at the top of my suspect list."

"Well, we didn't know that. Anyway, I need those sanitary towels before… Well, you know. The blood, and everything."

The blush creeps down Fergusson's neck. "You haven't answered my question."

"What question? I didn't hear a question, did you, Nora?"

I open my mouth, then think better of it. This approach may have worked for Mr Pender back at the police station, but here, no senior officer is going to burst in and break things up. Regardless, I eye the front door suspiciously.

"Why are you and your daughter interfering in my investigation?" Fergusson asks, frowning at Archie. Maybe he did want that biscuit after all.

"We're not, are we Nora? Who says we are?"

"It doesn't matter who, but I hear you've been asking questions about Paul Marshall and his daughter Karen Brown."

Mum feigns surprise. "Us? Why would we do that? We don't even know this Karen… What did you say? Brown, was it?"

Fergusson steps closer to Mum. "Stay out of my

investigation."

"Like I said, I don't know what you're talking about."

Fergusson stands suspiciously still, his eyes fixed just off to the side of Mum. I follow his gaze, as he reaches out and picks up a crumpled piece of paper. He turns, his eyes shining. "A betting slip from Rybrookes."

Paul Marshall's betting slip. I must have tossed it there when I emptied my pockets to wash my jeans.

"That's the bookmaker's Paul Marshall frequents." Fergusson takes a small plastic bag from his pocket and places the slip inside. "Now, how did that get here?"

"That's mine," Mum says.

"That's evidence tying you two to Paul Marshall. Did you and Paul plan the murder together?" The question is directed at me.

"I… I…" It really isn't what it looks like.

"I told you, it's mine. I like a flutter every now and then."

Fergusson nods. "So, it'll be your fingerprints we find, will it, Miss James? Not Nora's?"

It won't just be mine he finds, but Paul Marshall's too.

"Hers might be there, from moving the papers about." Mum sniffs. "She does that, shifts my stuff."

She makes me sound like a naughty child.

Fergusson pockets the evidence bag. "I'm sure the lab will tell me either way."

"Will a Yorkie do?" Mum asks, indicating Archie who sits by my feet, his head cocked to the side. Fergusson frowns. Mum explains with a sigh. "Instead of a lab." She attempts to hide her smirk.

Fergusson moves closer, backing Mum into the work surface. "Don't push me, Miss James."

"I'd like you to step back, now." Mum's voice is calm.

"Or what?"

"Or I'll encourage my client to press charges of false imprisonment." Mr Pender stands in the kitchen doorway, his mobile phone raised. "A case I'll happily take on pro bono."

Mum giggles. "I'm pro bono."

Fergusson steps back. Glaring, he pushes past Mr Pender and leaves, slamming the front door shut behind him.

I run to Mum, wrapping my arms around her. "Are you okay? What were you doing? You shouldn't antagonise him."

Mum grins. "That was Matty's idea."

I frown at him. "Yours? But, how…"

"When I saw Fergie at the door, I ducked into the bedroom and sent him a text. He told me what to do." Mum beams at her friend. "Worked a treat."

"Always does." Mr Pender indicates his mobile. "And this video should keep him off your backs for a while too."

Sometimes I could hug that man. "I worry about you two."

They grin.

Mum scoops her car keys out of the fruit bowl. "We'd best get going if we're—"

Mr Pender clamps his hands over his ears. "La la la la la. Not listening."

She plants a kiss on his cheek before heading for the car.

"Shouldn't we lock up first?" I ask.

"Matty will take care of it."

"He has a key?"

"Course, he waters my plants every year when I go to Ibiza. Well, he did, until you came back."

I try to imagine Mum enjoying the Spanish architecture, but it's impossible. Her dancing about covered in foam in Pacha, *that* I can imagine.

"Now you're home, Matty's coming with me."

I stare at her, trying to figure out if she's joking. Then decide I'd rather not know. "Who do you think told Fergusson about our investigation? The gambler or jumped-up wee madam?"

"My money's on Veitch, she's not a fan of yours."

"Shame, there was me thinking we could be friends."

She stares at me. "Nora, did you just make a joke?"

I smile. "You know, I think I did."

Mum grins. "You're starting to get the hang of this crazy cosy crime caper, aren't you?"

She's lost the plot, but then, I'm not sure she ever had the plot to begin with.

**

Veitch glares at us as we hurry past her office. I didn't expect her to be working, not at the weekend.

Mum waves. "Hi Babs, or is it Barbie?"

"Leave, or I'll call security."

Mum stops. "Now why would a nice, upmarket place like Calburn Court need security?"

"We've been targeted by two local criminals."

"Really?" Mum looks suddenly interested.

"Yes. So far, they're guilty of trespassing, theft, and possibly murder." She smirks in my direction. I think she knows about the wheelchair.

Mum doesn't miss a beat. "How awful. Do you hear that, Nora? We'd best check on Sammy, make sure he's all right." She hurries along the corridor, heading for the stairs.

Sammy is surprised by our arrival but welcomes us warmly. My bum has barely touched the couch before Mum sends me off with a brisk: "Tea, Nora."

Scowling, I head to the kitchen. This time I'm using salt. Unscrewing the top, I tip the contents of the shaker into the Hibs mug. Let's see if she can taste the 'sugar' this time. Trying my best to hide my smirk, I carry the tea through on a tray.

"Blackmail? You're sure?" Sammy asks.

Mum nods. "I'm afraid so."

Sammy shakes her head. He looks truly shocked. I'm

starting to think Mum was right, maybe Mrs Marshall really did like Sammy.

Mum picks up the floral cup.

"Oh, actually…" I gesture at the tray.

Sammy picks up the Hibernian mug.

"Well, that's…"

They slurp their tea. I close my eyes, awaiting the inevitable coughing and spluttering.

"Uh! Nora, did you forget the sugar again?"

I peek out of one partially-opened eyelid. Mum tuts and takes her tea back to the kitchen. Across from me, Sammy frowns down into his mug.

"Sorry, Sammy, I didn't mean—"

"Interesting taste, did you use the floral teabags? Never tried them before." He smacks his lips. "Not bad."

Good grief.

Mum returns with fresh tea and a pack of biscuits. She's certainly making herself at home. After helping herself to the first three biscuits, she offers the pack round. Sammy politely declines.

"Jamesina was always nice to me." He says, licking his lips. I do wish he'd stop that.

I take the biscuits from Mum before she finishes the packet. "Tell us about her."

"She was here about three years. We chatted from time to time, and I always saw lots of other residents visiting, giving her gifts, and… Ah…" Sammy's cheeks flush. "Maybe you're right about the blackmail."

"Did she give you anything other than your stick?" Mum somehow manages to form the words, her cheeks bulging with biscuits.

"Some hats and coats. You know, for birthdays and Christmas."

"Were they new?" I have a feeling I already know the answer.

"No, they belonged to an old gentleman friend of hers who'd passed."

"Do you know his name? Or what he looked like?" I'm guessing a full name and previous address are out of the question.

Sammy licks his lips again. I offer him his mug. He looks surprised.

"I thought you were thirsty." It sounds better than 'stop licking your lips, you look slimy'.

He wipes his mouth with a cloth hanky. "Medication. Makes the mouth water."

Mum nods, knowingly.

"She brought me a cake once too. Just the once mind. She was a fantastic baker." Sammy smiles.

I frown. I didn't know Mrs Marshall could bake. Not that I knew her, but I certainly didn't see any of the usual baking paraphernalia in her kitchen when I was searching for that basin. Perhaps that's why she was so keen to steal Mrs Baillie's recipes, so she could pass them off as her own. I dig deeper. "Did you ever ask her to bake you another?"

"All the time."

"But she refused?"

He nods and wipes a tear from his eye.

Of course, what's to say Mrs Marshall baked that cake? I glance at Mum. I can only think of one suspect who's known for her baking.

***

Knocking on Mrs Baillie's door, Mum pushes it open and yells her greeting. "Isabel, are you in?"

There's a clattering from the bedroom before a cupboard slams shut. Mrs Baillie emerges, her face flushed.

"Sorry, is this a bad time?" Even if it is, there's no way I'll get Mum to leave without some free cake.

"No, no. I was just getting some wool for a cardigan." Her hands are empty.

"Would you like some help?" I ask.

"Thank you, dear, but I'll get it later."

Something's wrong. Is someone here? Is she in trouble?

"Mrs Baillie, can you show me your roses, I'd like to see them close-up." Eyes wide, I flick my head towards the front door and offer her my hand.

She frowns before her face clears. "I'm okay, dear, I just got a fright. After what happened to Mrs Marshall…" She averts her gaze. "I'm afraid I…" Her cheeks flush. "Well, I have had children, you know."

My shoulders relax.

"Why don't you two put the kettle on and help yourself to some cake, I'll be through in a minute."

"You don't have to ask me twice." Mum heads for the kitchen, a spring in her step. That woman really does love cake.

I remain in the hall with Mrs Baillie. "I can get the wool for you, so you've got it for after."

She laughs. "I may be old, but I can still carry a few skeins, besides, I know the lot number. Go on, the cake won't slice itself."

Mum looks up guiltily as I enter the kitchen. There's a smudge of brown icing on the side of her mouth. Three large slices of coffee cake sit on plates.

"Sneaking an extra slice, were you?"

Eyes wide, her mouth opens in horror. "Nora Delilah James, I can't believe you would accuse your own mother of… of…"

I cringe at the use of my middle name. "It's McIntyre, remember?"

She adjusts her posture. "That doesn't make your insinuations any less insulting."

She's good. I almost feel guilty.

Suppressing a smile, I wipe the side of my mouth. Realisation flashes over Mum's face and her hand flies up to her cheek. "That's from breakfast."

I give a slow nod that I hope says: 'sure it is'.

She harrumphs. "Shut up and make the tea."

I can't help but chuckle. Mum picks up two of the plates and takes them through to the living room. Making sure she's gone, I help myself to a slither of cake. The smooth, buttery icing dissolves on my tongue. I close my eyes, savouring the flavour.

"I saw that." Mum stands in the doorway, hands on hips.

"I, eh…" Busted.

She grins. "Quick, snag me another bit."

"Is everything okay in there?" Mrs Baillie shouts through. We look up, our cheeks bulging. Mum dabs her mouth with a tea towel before handing it to me. It looks clean enough, or it did before Mum got icing all over it.

Hiding our crime as best we can, we carry the tea through. Mrs Baillie sits on her armchair, knitting. The wool is fuchsia. I knew it'd be pink.

"For my grandson." She informs us.

"Lovely." I hope I sound convincing.

Mrs Baillie smiles.

"Did you know Mrs Marshall passed one of your cakes off as her own?" Mum asks, blunt as ever. And lacking any proof.

"Of course, she did it many times."

Mum sits down. "And it didn't bother you?"

Mrs Baillie lowers her knitting. "Mrs Marshall wasn't very nice, dear. She had no respect for other people's things. Cakes, roses, you name it."

"So, why did you make her cakes?" I ask, helping myself to a mug of tea.

"Well, dear, for one thing, I like baking, and I can't eat it all myself."

"And for another?" I sip the tea.

Mrs Baillie sighs. "I guess I thought if I was nice to her, perhaps she'd stop being so horrid."

Mum stuffs the cake into her mouth. "So, she wasn't blackmailing you?"

That woman's as subtle as Mrs Baillie's wool.

"About what, dear?"

Neither of us has an answer for that, but, as usual, that doesn't stop Mum from trying. "Have you ever stolen anything? Or had an affair?"

I'm not sure Mum understands how blackmail works. If the victims just admit their secrets when asked, there wouldn't be anything to blackmail them with.

Miraculously, Mrs Baillie looks more amused than annoyed. Lucky really, I've eaten so much cake, I'm not sure I can move. Slumping back, I rub my stomach. It was worth it.

"No affairs, secret children, closeted lovers, or convictions. The worst thing I ever did was put off-milk in a friend's coffee."

This is a dead end. Mrs Baillie had no reason to murder Mrs Marshall.

Finishing our tea, we bid her farewell and wobble our way out.

We can strike Mrs Baillie from the MOO board. That just leaves Barbara Veitch, who's only on the board because I don't like her, and Paul Marshall, the only one with a motive. Guess that's that. Now all that's left is to find out his whereabouts on Monday night. Not sure he's going to tell us willingly, but we have to try. And if anyone can get him to talk, it's my mum.

"So, how are we going to get Paul Marshall to open up?"

Mum frowns, her eyes fixed on Mrs Marshall's house. Her mouth curls into a smile. That can't be good.

"We blackmail him."

Yep, I was right. "Blackmail him? With what?"

"Whatever we find in there." She points to Mrs Marshall's.

Oh no, not again.

She brushes cake crumbs from her clothes. "No time like the present."

Any time but the present.

Glancing around, looking very shifty, Mum approaches Mrs Marshall's bungalow and takes the rubber cover off the key safe.

"What was the number again?"

What? Not breaking in this time? "1934."

The code works. Clearly, Ms Veitch isn't *that* worried about security. So much for hiring guards and all that nonsense. There's not even a police presence or tape. Maybe that's just something that happens on TV. Or maybe they got everything they need from here already.

Mrs Marshall's house is sparser than I remember. They must have started preparing it for a new tenant. Makes sense, there's probably a waiting list for a place like this. Maybe that's why Karen was here, to see what all had to be removed.

The equipment remains in the corner of the living room, but the dresser and all the ornaments are gone. Funny, there's still a shawl on the back of the armchair, and a half-eaten box of chocolates on the floor.

Frowning, I head to the kitchen. Several of the cupboards lie open, their contents removed. The crockery's gone, and the cutlery. But the collection of magnets remains on the fridge. Something doesn't feel right. I march to the bedroom, Mum following close behind. Mrs Marshall's clothes are heaped on her bed and the floor below. The antique dressing table and wardrobe are gone. A few scattered pieces of jewellery — including the gold locket she accused me of stealing — are visible through the chaos. Nobody would clear a house this way.

"She's taken what she can sell."

"Who?" Mum asks.

"Karen, who else." So much for her not needing the money.

Mum picks up a yellow blouse and holds it against herself. "Hefty lass." She tosses it back on the bed. "This is good."

I gesture at the chaos. "How can this be good?"

"Because she wasn't looking for paperwork and we are."

"What about bank statements, things to blackmail people with? That's paperwork."

Mum waves away my concerns. "If you're after paperwork, you wouldn't make such a mess. That reduces your chances of finding it. The only stuff that's missing is the obvious stuff. But she's missed a few good pieces. Some of these clothes are designer, she'd get a good few pennies for them."

She may have a point. I lift aside a bundle of clothes, exposing a red Dior handbag. "Is that…"

Lifting it, Mum sniffs the leather. "It's real."

I gasp. That bag's worth over three thousand pounds. "It wasn't Karen. Someone else has been here."

Mum nods. "My money's on Paul. And I bet the local pawn shop staff will be able to identify him. Would you recognise the furniture?"

I shake my head. "I was barely in here."

Mum sighs. Okay, back to Plan A. Start digging. If Mrs Marshall's anything like me, she'll keep her important documents in her knicker drawer."

"Good to know." I grin. "Where do you stash the Dairy Milk?" I *know* she moved her chocolate cache after offering me some.

Mum glares. "Nice try. My money, you can have. Touch my chocolate and you're out on your ear."

Chuckling, I lift some clothes from the floor and scream.

"What? What? Was it a spider?" Mum crawls onto the bed. "Oh god, don't say it was a spider."

"Hand."

"What?"

Vomit ejects from my mouth, splattering down onto the open palm.

CHAPTER TWENTY

The paramedic wraps a grey blanket around my shoulders. It smells musty, I think they found it in Mrs Marshall's house.

I sit on the steps outside, cradling a cup of sweet tea. Mum's inside, making a nuisance of herself. Her voice drifts out the open door. "Definitely dead then? Are you sure? Only, you seem a little young… Fine, fine, I'll get out of your way… Are there any wounds… Well, why can't I? It's not like you're going to bring him back."

Him.

"Oi! Get off." Mum harrumphs and drops down beside me. "I've been asked to leave."

"What did you do?"

"Nothing."

I stare at her.

She sighs. "I was only trying to get a closer look. How was I supposed to know I'd trip and push the paramedic on top of the body?"

It'd be funny under other circumstances.

Mum wraps her arm around my shoulder. "Are you all right?"

"Who was he?"

There's a pause before she responds. "It's Paul Marshall."

Paul?

"Guess we were wrong about him."

I stare at her. Did she just say that?

Mum returns my stare, her expression blank. Sighing, I ask the inevitable. "How…"

"I was hoping you could tell me that." DI Buchanan stands before us, notebook in hand. "Two dead bodies in one week, and both discovered by you."

Mum bristles. "Who called the fuzz?"

"We received a call from a concerned neighbour who reported an incident at the property of one Miss Marian James."

"Meaning Mrs Emerson over the road spotted the police presence and wanted the gossip."

"I can't comment on that, Miss James."

Mum sniffs. "Your comrade, Tom Fergusson, paid us a call. A threatening one."

Buchanan nods. "So I gather from your solicitor."

Mum squares her shoulders. "My solicitor has no right speaking to you without my permission. Why were you calling him anyway? Us Jameses can look after ourselves."

"Actually, Mr Pender was in the property when I arrived to investigate your neighbour's concerns."

I frown, either DI Buchanan was very fast to respond, or…

"Matty was still there?"

"Yes. I believe Mr Pender was, and I quote," He flicks back a page in his notebook. "Grabbing a bit of nosh."

Mum chuckles. "He always did like my cooking."

Seriously, what is going on between Mum and Mr Pender?

"So," Mum glares at the DI, all traces of her earlier humour gone. "You thought you'd best find us and warn us not to press charges."

"If you wish to press charges, you are entitled to do

so."

"But?" Mum's voice remains stern.

The policeman sighs and crouches down to our level. "May I be honest with you?"

I nod.

Mum scoffs. "I highly doubt it."

Buchanan lowers his gaze and stands. "So, you found another body…"

"We both found this one." Mum sounds almost ecstatic.

"And how did you come to be in that particular house?"

"I used the key," Mum says triumphantly. "It's not breaking and entering if you use the key."

Please stop talking.

To my surprise, DI Buchanan smiles before suppressing it. His gaze shifts to me. "How are you, Mrs McIntyre?"

"Cold." Excellent answer, Nora. That didn't sound silly at all.

Buchanan nods. "It's the shock."

"It's hardly her first dead body." Mum scoffs.

"No, but it can still catch us off-guard."

"The hand… It was like…" Like Colin's. I bury my head in the blanket. An arm encircles me. I allow myself to be pulled into a soft body and smell Mum's familiar perfume. Coty L'Aimant.

"It's okay, I'm here." Her voice sounds muffled. A strong hand briefly grips my shoulder. When I peek out from the blanket, DI Buchanan is gone.

"Come on, let's get you home."

"But the police…"

"They know where to find you." Mum pulls me to my feet and leads me towards the car park.

As we round the corner, Barbara Veitch strides towards us. "You two, I should have known. If the police weren't already here, I'd be phoning them myself."

"Everything all right here?" DI Buchanan stands behind us. I hadn't heard him approach.

Veitch's eyes narrow. "You again? Haven't I answered enough questions?"

"All but my last, Ms Veitch. Is everything all right?"

"No, it isn't." She treats him to one of her famous glares. "What gives you the right to enter one of our properties without asking permission?"

Buchanan raises an eyebrow. "Permission from whom, Ma'am? I understand the resident in question, one Mrs Jamesina Marshall, is deceased."

"Permission from me. Don't you think I have a right to know what's going on at my own complex?"

"If you insist." He doesn't sound amused. "Miss James and Mrs McIntyre have discovered a body."

Veitch scoffs. "That was days ago."

"Another body, Ma'am."

She sighs. "The residents are old, Inspector. If we phoned you lot every time one of them popped their clogs, you'd never be away from here."

Charming.

"I'm afraid it looks a little more serious than that, Miss V—"

"It's Ms," Mum says. "Like the bee. Msssss."

Veitch throws Mum a glare, but Buchanan simply nods. "Please return to your office, I'll be by to interview you in due course."

Veitch almost bobs a curtsy as she scurries back to the complex.

Buchanan walks around us, blocking our path. "Leaving the scene of a crime?" He sounds serious, but I swear there's a hint of humour in those blue eyes.

"I'm taking Nora. She's in shock, needs a cuppa."

"I believe the paramedics already supplied her with one."

Mum scoffs. "You call that cloudy dishwater, tea?"

He smiles. "You should try the stuff we get at the station."

"I have, many times."

Buchanan raises an eyebrow. That's it, Mum, admit to being a repeat offender. That'll get him to believe us.

"No doubt Nora has too," Mum adds. "Right before your crony attacked our solicitor."

Buchanan sighs. "PC Fergusson's been having… issues, at home."

"Oh, that makes it all right then," Mum says with a scoff.

They lock eyes. I almost feel sorry for Buchanan.

Mum looks away, blushing. You've got to be kidding me.

"All right, Miss James, you can take Mrs McIntyre home. I'll be round at eleven tomorrow morning to take your statements." Buchanan steps aside, allowing us to pass.

"It's Nora." My voice is shaky.

He nods. "Andrew."

"Thanks, Andrew." Heat rushes to my cheeks as Mum pulls me out of earshot.

"Why, Nora McIntyre, I do believe you were flirting."

I'm too tired to argue. I'm even too tired to roll my eyes. Since when were good manners considered flirting? That's certainly not how Mum flirts. She thrusts her bosoms at them. Not that I have bosoms to thrust, more, slight symmetrical rises in my jumper. And not that I was flirting. Or had any desire to do so. Oh lord, thank goodness Mum can't read my thoughts, she would be commenting something about protesting too much.

I allow Mum to assist me into the car and to put my seatbelt on. I hear her door slam and stare out the passenger-side window as we drive home.

Paul Marshall. Dead.

"Are you getting out?"

The engine's off. Frowning, I glance around. We're in

the car park of The Moorpond. "I thought we were going home."

She unfastens her seatbelt. "Like I told the dishy detective, you need tea. And where better to get that than here?" She exits the car before I can protest.

Freddie is serving a group of inebriated men who sway and wrap their arms around each other's heads while singing a variety of inappropriate songs.

"Oi, oi, totty's arrived." They leer at a young waitress in a tight camel-coloured t-shirt.

Without a word, Freddie blasts them with the soda dispenser. "Manners please, there are ladies present."

I'm starting to warm to Freddie.

"Give them room." He flicks his dish rag at them. Muttering and shaking off the soda, they step aside.

Yes, definitely warming to him.

"Good evening, ladies. What'll it be?" He runs the cloth over the bar.

"The usual Freddie."

"A large one, Marian?"

"I can give you a large one." The men laugh, slapping the speaker on the back. I can't believe someone bet Mum to an innuendo. Mum looks them up and down, she doesn't seem impressed.

"A very large one please, Freddie," Mum says with a sniff.

The men roar again. Freddie shakes his head. "And for you, miss?"

"Mrs." Because that's so important right now, Nora. "Tea please, lots of sugar."

"Grab a seat, ladies. I'll bring your drinks over."

Mum plonks herself down at a nearby table and sighs. "Paul bloomin' Marshall."

My thoughts exactly. "Do you know how…"

She shakes her head. "Didn't get to see much, the paramedics kept getting in the way."

I nod.

"But I didn't see any blood."

I nod again. "Maybe a heart attack then?"

"Sure…"

Freddie arrives with the drinks as Mum continues. "And as he's having the heart attack, he pulls a bunch of clothes off the bed, completely covering himself."

"Meaning…" I whisper, not wanting the barman to overhear.

Freddie pulls out a vacant chair, spins it around, and joins us at the table. I stare at him in surprise.

"A few clothes, sure, that could happen. But managing to not show even the tiniest bit of himself…" Mum takes a swig of her cola.

"So, what? You're saying it's…"

Another murder.

CHAPTER TWENTY-ONE

Another murder? But that would mean… "Paul Marshall was innocent." The words are out before I can even wonder whether we should be discussing this in front of Freddie.

"Or there are two killers."

I slurp my tea. Two killers. It's possible, I suppose. But who would want to kill Paul Marshall? The loan sharks? But he's no good to them dead. An accident perhaps? A threat that was taken too far. But Mum said there wasn't any blood. Surely loan sharks would inflict damage first.

Maybe Barbara Veitch had finally had enough of him. No, she looked genuinely shocked. Then again, she could have just been surprised that we found the body so quickly.

I suddenly realise both Mum and Freddie are staring at me. "The tea is very good, thank you."

Freddie nods and rests his chin on the back of the chair. I make eyes at Mum and flick my head in his direction. Mum ignores me.

"Problem is, with Paul Marshall dead, how do we prove he did or didn't kill—"

"Maybe we should talk about this later." I smile at

Freddie. "How's business?"

They both stare at me blankly. I give up. "What's Freddie doing here?"

"He works here." Mum gestures around the room.

"At this table. What's he doing at this table?"

"He's waiting to give us info, away from that rowdy crowd."

"How does Freddie know what we're doing?"

Mum reddens. "Oh look, there's Mrs Emerson." She waves enthusiastically and grabs her drink. "She'll be wanting an update."

I slap my hand down onto her arm before she can make her escape. "What did you do?"

"Nothing."

"Then answer the question."

"Nora, it's rude to keep Mrs Emerson waiting."

"You don't even like Mrs Emerson."

"I might. Maybe. If I spent some time with her. I'll give it a go."

"Mum." I fix her with my hardest glare. She doesn't look remotely fazed, but I continue to stare.

Finally, she sighs and drops back down onto the seat. "Fine. I may have posted it on my 'gram."

I blink. Her what? I must look suitably blank because Freddie explains. "She means her Instagram account. Social media."

Soc... "You posted, on social media, that we're interfering in a police investigation?"

"Course not." She scoffs. "I posted about how we're going to clear your name. If we happen to catch the killer at the same time, then that's just a coincidence."

"A coincidence? We've been trying to clear my name by finding the murderer. There's no coincidence about it."

She sniffs. "Potato tomato."

"That's still not— How could you do something so stupid?"

"Stu— What a way to speak to your mother. I raised

you better than that."

The hysterical laugh escapes before I can stop it. "Raised me. I'd hardly call it that. You were too busy raising a glass, among other things."

Anger and pain flash through her eyes. Snatching her arm away, she stomps out of the bar.

Sucking a breath in between his teeth, Freddie gets to his feet and tucks in the vacant chairs.

I shouldn't have said that. Freddie picks up Mum's drink. She looked crushed. He wipes the table. I didn't mean it. He stands, staring down at me. Eyes stinging, I meet his gaze. He remains silent. I sigh. "You don't need to say it, I know."

"The bit about Marian, maybe. But not the rest."

My shoulders slump. As if it matters now. "Thanks, Freddie but I just want to go home."

"To Marian's?"

I wince. Dropping a fiver onto the table, I make my exit. Mum's car's still in the car park. Frowning, I look around, finally spotting her at the far end of the beer garden sitting on the stone wall that borders the woods.

Lowering my head, I walk over, my hands in my pockets. "Sorry, Mum."

"Me too."

"That wasn't fair."

"I'm trying, Nora."

"I know."

She turns, her eyes glistening. "I got a second shot, even if you didn't want me to. And I'm doing okay, aren't I?"

"Better than okay." A lump forms in my throat. "I couldn't... If you hadn't..."

Freddie circles the tables, looking for non-existent glasses to clear. Mum chuckles. "Come on, let's put him out of his misery."

Smiling, we walk over. Mum waves a greeting. "Freddie my friend, what's the word?"

"I'm sure I wouldn't know."

"Come on now Freddie, we both know you've got something to say."

"I say lots of things." He wipes crisp crumbs from a picnic table.

"Things you've been paid to say?" Mum asks, her eyes narrowing.

"Sometimes."

"And what were you paid to say?"

"I'm no answering machine."

"But you've got a message?"

"Might do."

This has gone on long enough. I unclip my necklace and lower it onto the table, each link sounding its worth.

"What's Freddie going to do with that?" Mum asks.

"It's not even my style." He sounds genuinely offended.

"Sell it, I don't care, just tell us what you know."

Mum takes hold of my arm, pulling me aside. "That's not how we do things here."

"Since when? You're always suggesting I bribe people and the one time I try…"

"Freddie and I have an understanding."

Oh lord, please don't let that be a euphemism.

We turn back to Freddie, who's nudging the necklace with one suspicious finger. Mum picks up the offending item and hands it back to me. "All right Freddie, how about I promise to stop cheating at darts?"

Freddie sighs, crossing his arms. Mum pouts, considering. "What if I agree to stop sneaking behind the bar and changing the menu to things from the Urban Dictionary?"

He holds his stance. No deal.

"What if I promise to wear knickers under my snakeskin mini-skirt?"

Take the deal, Freddie, take the deal!

"Och, fine. I promise to stop hosting Topless Tuesdays

and Thong Thursdays when you're on holiday."

Freddie unfolds his arms. Looks like we have a deal.

"Lady phoned, asked you to meet her at four. Said you'd know where."

"What did she sound like?"

"A lady."

Mum frowns. "Young?"

"Younger than you."

"Pretty?"

How can someone sound pretty? Next, she'll be asking what colour hair it sounded like she had.

"If you like that type."

Mum considers. "Did she sound overly skinny?"

Oh, for heaven's sake, what a question.

Freddie raises his eyebrows and heads back to the bar. Mum claps her hands together. "Sounds like Veitch is ready to talk."

"Won't it look suspicious, us suddenly reappearing?"

"No problem, we just need that wheelchair and our wigs."

She's lost it, she's actually lost it.

"Besides, we have to go back. Murderers always return to the scene of the crime."

Murd… She does know we didn't kill anyone, doesn't she?

***

For once, luck seems to be on my side. Not only do I manage to persuade Mum to leave her wig in the car, but the police are too busy to take any notice of us as we scurry towards the main complex.

Barbara Veitch doesn't look happy to see us. She ushers us into her office and closes the door. "Don't sit. Just stand. Over there." She gestures towards a bare wall at the far end of the room. She looks mad. Should I be worried that she's blocking our only exit?

"I'd rather sit." I step towards the chair.

"No. Just. The wall."

I glance at Mum, trying to figure out how to signal a pincer movement. Assuming she'd know what that is. What am I saying, she probably uses it to trap her victims, or as she calls them, dates.

I step to the right. Mum steps to the right. What is she doing? I flick my fingers, trying to subtly signal her to move the other way. She stares down at my hand, then up at me, frowning.

"Did you just break wind? Really, Nora. Of all the times to break wind. There aren't even proper windows in here. Open the door, Veitch. Quick, before we all pass out."

Thanks, Mum. I sigh. "Do as she says. Open the door and step out of the way. We want to leave." Where are the police when you need them?

Mum frowns. "No, we don't."

"Yes, we do." I hiss.

"No, we don't." Mum glares at me. "We want to know what Barbie here has to tell us. Remember?"

"And we will, but we have that… thing." Excellent Nora, smooth as ever. To drive my message home, I widen my eyes and flick my head in the direction of the door.

"What thing? Smutty Book Club?"

"Yes…" I struggle to even say the words. "Smutty Book Club, we'll be late."

"Since when were you interested in Smutty Book Club? I thought you preferred historical fiction."

"No, no, I can't wait to go."

Mum frowns. "It's not until half six. How long do you need to get ready?"

I sigh again, defeated. "Get it over with, Veitch. Just kill us. Her first."

Mum has the cheek to look offended. If she'd picked up on my signals, we would've been out of here by now.

"Kill you? Why would I…" Veitch shakes her head.

"Perhaps if your Mum really had soiled my hand-sewn cushions… Luckily for you, she seems to have been mistaken."

I frown. "You were trying to get us against a wall."

"I'm not letting either of you near my fabrics."

That's fair. "You're blocking the door."

"I'm stopping anyone from interrupting us."

Ah, well, she may have a point. "So, can I sit?"

"No!" Veitch practically springs forward. I jump back, colliding with a potted plant, knocking soil onto the cream carpet. Veitch's eyes widen, then narrow. I think she may have changed her mind about not killing us.

"This. Is a new carpet."

"It's lovely, very… cream." I look at Mum, silently pleading with her to rescue me. For once, she seems to pick up on my cue.

"Yes, very cream. It goes with the cream walls and ceiling."

That's not helping.

"Which," She adds "Goes well with the brown door and desk… and soil."

I'm starting to see where I get my way with words.

Mum scans the room. "Have you thought of adding some colour? Other than the child's paintings, I mean. To show off your personality." Her gaze rests on Veitch. "Ah… Maybe get a personality first."

Veitch visibly stiffens. Yep, she's definitely reconsidering her options. Thankfully, there doesn't seem to be any obvious murder weapons lying around, like ropes, lead pipes, or candlesticks. Just the letter opener. Maybe the power cord for the computer. Then again, Veitch is freakishly strong, she might not need a weapon.

Dropping to my knees, I attempt to scoop up the soil and return it to the pot. The muck refuses to comply, instead, burying itself in the carpet in some weird game of hide and seek.

"Stop that. Just—" Veitch composes herself before

finishing her sentence. "Leave it, it's fine. Just stand over there." She gestures to the other side of the room, nearer the desk.

Getting to my feet, I wipe the soil from my jeans. It's only as the minuscule brown specks scatter over the carpet that I realise my faux pas.

Grabbing Mum by the arm, I pull her over to where Veitch has banished us, and eye the desk. She's messed up this time. If she does try anything, she's going to have to beat me to that letter opener. And by me, I mean Mum. It looks like solid silver. There's no way Mum hasn't clocked it.

"So, how can we help you, Ms Veitch." I sound as polite as I'd hoped. The last thing I need is to upset her any further.

"Yeah, hurry up, Veitch. Nora needs time to scrub up for Smutty Book Club." Mum pulls the office chair towards her and drops down onto it before I can stop her. Veitch's hands clench into fists. I grab Mum's shoulder, trying to pull her up. She bats me away. "Behave, Nora. Go stand over there." She gestures in the general direction of the potted plant. Very funny.

Mum flicks idly through some loose papers. "For a put-together woman, your desk's a mess."

Veitch steps forward, slapping her hand on top of Mum's, fixing it in place.

"Leave them."

Their eyes lock.

"I will. As soon as you tell us why you summoned us here."

She steps back, releasing Mum's hand. One nil to Mum.

Veitch's shoulders visibly slump. "It's about Paul." Her slender fingers select a torn scrap of paper, she hands it to Mum who frowns down at it before passing it to me.

"I found it on my desk after…"

I'm surprised she found anything under all that mess. I read: 'I'm sorry, I just wanted the money. They were going to kill me. I had no choice.'

It's unsigned, but the meaning is clear. A confession. Paul Marshall killed his mother to save his own skin. But he didn't inherit, Karen did, and 'they' — whoever 'they' are — must have killed Paul.

I stare at the paper, the words becoming unfocused. It's over. No more suspicion, no more police… The police. "Why didn't the police take this?"

Veitch looks away. "I found it after that DI finished questioning me."

Mum snatches the note, pushes Veitch aside and marches out of the complex. I scurry after her.

DI Buchanan is exiting Mrs Marshall's as we approach. Mum strides up to him, waving the confession in the air. "Oi, Andy, I've got something for you."

I bet it's not the first time she's said that.

Buchanan frowns. Mum wafts the paper under his nose. "A confession."

He raises an eyebrow. "Yours?"

"Very funny." She hands it over, barely giving him time to read it before continuing. "Like I said, my Nora had nothing to do with it. You can get your lapdog to back off."

"Miss James, I can assure you—"

"Save it. Your pretty-boy charm doesn't wash with me. You're a cop. Full stop."

"I'm hardly a boy, Miss James."

At least he didn't take out his handcuffs and chase her around the grounds. I shudder at the thought, knowing how much Mum would enjoy it.

Buchanan takes a pair of reading glasses from the inner pocket of his suit, inspecting the note more closely. "Thank you for bringing this to my attention."

"That's it?" She places her hands firmly on her hips. "No apology?"

He removed his glasses, his face serious. "This is a crime scene, Miss James, unless you and your daughter wish to give your statements now, I suggest you leave." He returns the glasses to his pocket. "I'll be sure to have this analysed." He turns his back, dismissing us.

"Analysed? What's to analyse? I've given you a suspect, a motive, and a confession. Isn't that enough?"

Buchanan sighs. "You'll forgive me for questioning an unsigned confession handed to me by the prime suspect's mother."

Mum visibly deflates. Buchanan seems to take pity on her. "The lab boys can analyse the handwriting and confirm if it is that of the deceased. Once we have that, we may broaden our enquiries. Now please Miss James, go home."

Nodding, Mum obeys, almost meekly. Bobbing a curtsy — and wondering why on earth I just did that — I follow.

She walks in silence, her steps heavy. Closing her car door with a light click, she starts the engine and reverses out of the parking space.

As the town rolls by, people turn, waving at the familiar car, but Mum ignores their greetings. She doesn't even switch the radio on. Her eyes remain fixed straight ahead.

Pulling into the driveway, she unlocks the front door and heads for the kitchen. I stop in the vestibule, bending down to ruffle Archie's fur.

Mr Pender descends the stairs, a multicoloured towel wrapped around his waist. He's dripping wet. Averting my gaze, I hurry to fill the kettle.

We came back here after our visit to The Moorpond. I showered, and walked Archie. When did Mr Pender return? And why?

He follows me into the kitchen, not bothering to dress first. Should I offer him tea?

Mum's sitting at the kitchen table, she looks miserable. "We had it, Matty. Everything we needed to clear Nora's name. But Buchanan's not buying it."

Mr Pender perches on a chair, drying his hair. Please let that be a different towel.

"Buchanan's meticulous. He'd never prosecute without listening to the defence."

I place the biscuit tin on the table, Mum ignores it.

"We handed him a written confession, what more does he want?"

"The suspect to confess verbally."

"Can't. He's dead."

Mr Pender wipes water droplets from his glasses. "This confession, could it be accepted without any reasonable doubt?"

I place three cups of tea on the table. "Do you take milk, Mr Pender?"

He grins. "I think we can do away with the formalities, don't you, Nora?"

Given that he's sitting before me in nothing but a towel…

Mum sprinkles sugar into a cup. I'd already added two heaped spoonfuls, but don't have the heart to tell her. She slurps her tea, grimacing. "It wasn't signed."

"Has the handwriting been confirmed as being that of the suspect?"

"No." Mum ladles more sugar into her tea.

Mr Pender lowers the towel to his lap. "Marian…"

"I know, I know."

Pulling out a chair, I join them at the table, being careful to keep my gaze away from Mr Pender, in case that towel isn't providing full coverage.

Mum sighs. "I was starting to enjoy all that detective malarkey."

"You could always become a P.I." Mr Pender offers her a biscuit.

"Don't encourage her." No, really, don't. "She gets in enough trouble as it is."

"That's all right, she's got a good solicitor." He winks. I turn away as he stands.

"Best get going, I've got a date." He heads for the stairs. I open my mouth to ask Mum what's going on, but the look on her face stops me. Oh, no. Please, no. She's beaming. She's taking Mr Pender's passing comment seriously.

"I could you know."

No, you couldn't.

"It's not a bad idea."

It's a terrible idea.

"Nobody would suspect a middle-aged woman of being a sleuth."

Middle-aged? Maybe a decade ago. And why wouldn't they suspect a middle-aged woman of being a sleuth? Jane Marple, Agatha Raisin, Jessica Fletcher, Hetty Wainthropp. Okay, so they're fictional, but still…

"I bet loads of people would hire me."

Nobody will hire her. She's probably committed half the crimes in town.

"Do you think you need specific qualifications to be a P.I?"

"I… I…" I don't know what to say.

Mum slaps the table. "I'm going to look it up."

Wonderful.

Mr Pender sticks his head around the doorway. "See you later, Nora."

"Bye Mr Pender, Matty." And thanks for putting such a stupid idea in Mum's head.

***

The next morning, I wash and dress early, donning my best dress, the navy Ted Baker with the floral print.

Mum's tapping away on her ancient laptop when I enter the kitchen. Archie sits on the seat opposite, clearly hoping for some stray crumbs.

"Morning, Mum."

Silence.

"Good morning."

More silence.

"Mind if I borrow the car? Of course not, Nora, help yourself. Gee, thanks, Mum."

Nothing.

I lean over her shoulder. "You're serious then?"

"Why not? Don't you think I'd be good at it?"

Careful, Nora. "I… just didn't realise you were serious, that's all." Well dodged.

"Why wouldn't I be?"

Another trap. "I… don't know."

Mum's eyes narrow.

You've got this, Nora. "You don't like the police, why would you want to be one?" Good save.

"But that's the thing, I wouldn't be police. I'd be better. Fewer rules and all the fun." Her eyes sparkle with excitement.

"Sounds great." I hope I sound convincing.

She grins. "You look nice. Got a date?"

"No, I thought I'd try the Job Centre again."

"On a Sunday?"

I shrug. "The benefits of a small town."

Her eyes narrow. "If you say so. What about Hall-In? You fed up wiping bums already?"

I shake my head. I can't bring myself to ask Debbie for my job back, not after everything that's happened. "Mind if I take the car?"

"Help yourself, but I'll need it back by ten, I want to pick up a new camera before that DI comes round for our statements."

"No problem." I grab the keys.

Karen's not at the Job Centre when I arrive, no surprise there. The queue is long, but I should still be back in plenty of time. As they wait, the jobseekers share gossip.

"Did you hear there were gangland hitmen in town?"

"Tara down at the bank saw them, guns and all."

"You think they killed his mother too?"

"I heard she was strangled with her own underwear."

Have these rumours spread through Calburn Court?

Must be upsetting, not knowing what's going on. I know Mrs Marshall wasn't strangled. I know Paul Marshall wasn't shot. Well, I'm pretty sure he wasn't.

"Next." A young, blonde girl looks over.

"That's you," I say to a spotty lad in torn jeans, and head for the car.

Within minutes, I'm back at Calburn Court. There's no sign of the police presence that dominated the gardens yesterday. I head inside the main complex, rushing past Barbara Veitch who's walking a resident along the corridor.

"Hold on—"

"No time." I take the stairs. After the first flight, I wish I'd opted for the lift. Descending is so much easier. Wheezing, I haul myself up using the banister for support. At the next level, I exit the stairwell and puff my way along the corridor. At the far side, I find my prize. The lift doors greet me with silence.

As the doors squeak open, I step forwards, then back, as an elderly lady in an electric wheelchair drives out of the lift, catching me in the knee. Hobbling, I smile my apology. The woman glares in response and continues on her way. Thank goodness Mum didn't borrow one of those things from Mrs McGinty. If she had, there'd probably be a lot more bodies for the police to examine.

I press the button. Let's hope Sammy's home. The doors creak and begin to close. Pale, slender fingers force it open. Barbara Veitch glares at me. How did she get here so fast? She's not even winded.

"Why are you here?" She growls.

"Just visiting."

"Alone?" She looks around the otherwise empty lift.

"Yes."

Her eyes narrow.

"Do you mind, Mr McAllister's expecting me." Please don't follow me up. Please don't follow me up.

"Is that right?"

"Yes." No.

"Just you?"

"Yes." I try to sound offended. Veitch isn't buying it. Come on Nora, you can do this. You're a— You were, a James. "He's painting a… well, a painting… For Mum. For her birthday."

Veitch folds her arms, her foot stopping the lift door from closing.

What would Mum do? I suppress a smile, composing myself as best I can. "It's a nude portrait actually. I've got the pictures on my phone if you'd like a sneak peek."

Veitch's expression changes for the slightest second. "You have naked pictures of your mum, on your phone."

"Yes, it was surprisingly easy. I took her bra shopping and while she was changing, I stuck the phone through the curtain and, hey presto. Took a while to make sure I had enough angles." I take my mobile from my bag. "Some of them are rather artistic. The lighting was great, but then, it was a high-end retailer." I flick through my pictures. "Ah, here it is." I turn the phone around. Veitch steps back. The doors click shut. Thank goodness she didn't want a closer look. And thank goodness for Google.

Sammy answers the door on the second ring. His hair is dishevelled, and his robe lies open, exposing red tartan pyjamas below. "Nora?"

"Sorry for waking you Sammy, do you have a second?"

He steps back, granting me entrance. "It'll cost you."

I pause. Please don't say something creepy.

Sammy smiles. "Stick the kettle on, would you, love." He shuffles off towards the living room. I head for the kitchen. When I return with two cups of tea, Sammy's hair is smartly combed, and his robe is tied. "So…" He takes a cup from me. "How can I help?"

Placing my mug on a side table, I sit across from him. "I heard rumours, about Jamesina and her son. I know she was important to you, and I didn't want you to hear them and get upset."

Sammy slurps his tea. "Thanks, love, that means a lot."

"The truth is, Paul Marshall killed his mother for the inheritance. But he wasn't her beneficiary and his debtors caught up with him." I squeeze his hand. "I'm sorry I can't tell you more."

There's much frowning as Sammy processes what I've said. After ten minutes or so of general chit-chat, I head for Mrs Baillie's.

My phone rings as I exit the complex and I pull it from my bag.

"Did you start a shift or something?" Mum asks.

"Not quite, I got a little side-tracked." I glance at my watch. "I thought you didn't need the car until ten."

"I don't. Why? Where have you wandered off to? You sure you've not got a date?"

"No, I just… stopped off to see a friend."

"Is that what they call it now?"

"Mum…"

She laughs. "Okay, okay. Matty called, he said the post-mortem's back on Paul Marshall."

"That was quick."

"Well, apparently there was a rather noticeable puncture mark on his neck."

"He was stabbed?"

"Better. He was drugged."

Drugged? How is that better?

"I forget the names, but Matty said he was given a sedative, then a drug used to euthanise animals. Not sure if that was someone's idea of a joke."

"Do they still suspect loan sharks?"

"No idea. But he did say that the police are trying to track them down."

At least that's something.

"So, this date…"

I sigh. "There is no date."

"Well, the non-date then, is it with a certain DI Andrew Buchanan by any chance?"

"What? No."

"Ah, but you don't deny there's a date."

I sigh again. "I did deny it. Look, I've got to go. I'll be back soon." Hanging up, I walk down the short path towards Mrs Baillie's. There's police tape outside Mrs Marshall's but thankfully, no police presence. I wasn't looking forward to answering more questions.

I knock on the door. Hearing a mumbled voice call from inside, I enter. "Hello? Mrs Baillie? It's Nora."

"In the kitchen, dear." She smiles a greeting as I approach. "I'm afraid I've only just put the cake in."

"Thanks, but it's a little early for me." She must be confusing me with Mum.

"You go sit down. I'll pop the kettle on."

I do as instructed. There are fresh roses on a side table in the living room. Walking over, I inhale their scent.

"Here we are." She places a small tray on the coffee table.

"These are beautiful, did you grow them yourself?"

"Not those ones, they were a gift from Ryan, to apologise again about the dog droppings."

"He's a good lad."

"Very. So, to what do I owe this honour?"

I sit down and help myself to a cup of tea. "I was visiting Sammy McAllister and thought I'd stop by."

"That was nice of you, dear. How's little Archibald settling in?"

"He's great."

"I'm glad he's found a good home."

"Actually, it was Mrs Marshall I wanted to speak to you about."

Mrs Baillie picks up her knitting. "I hope you're not planning on tracking down a mob hitman, dear. I don't think that'd be very safe."

"No, definitely not." I pause. "Did you see them? The hitmen?"

She chuckles. "Something else I must have missed, I'm

afraid."

"Did you see Paul Marshall coming and going from his Mum's house over the last few days?"

"Yes, he was clearing out the furniture. Ms Veitch was helping. There have been some potential residents coming and going too. Although, none in rosé wigs."

I smile. "That's a shame. Did you see or hear anything yesterday?"

"No, dear. Did you?"

"No. It must have happened before we arrived."

"Must it, dear? That's very clever of you to know."

I frown. Surely we would have heard something if it'd happened while we were here. It couldn't have been a quiet attack, what with the mess in the bedroom. But then clothes being thrown don't make much noise, certainly not enough to have been heard through a wall. You'd be lucky to hear them in the hallway outside. But there must have been a struggle. They'd have had to incapacitate Paul Marshall in order to inject him. Unless he wasn't expecting the attack.

I shudder. Paul Marshall could have been fighting for his life on the other side of the wall while Mum and I were sitting eating cake. If we hadn't stayed so long, we might have seen the killer. And if we had…

I gulp down the tea, burning my throat.

"Are you all right, dear?"

"Perfectly." What if they'd still been in the house when Mum and I broke in? We could be lying dead with no one even looking for us.

"Are you sure? You look a little pale."

How long do bodies take to smell? Is that when they'd notice?

"Nora?"

I meet Mrs Baillie's gaze. I have to think of something else. "What kind of cake are you making?"

"My favourite, a Victoria sponge. Would you like some when it's done?"

Don't be sick, don't be sick. "No, thank you."

"I guess your investigation is over now, dear?"

I clasp my empty mug. "Yes."

"I rather thought you were enjoying yourselves."

My laugh sounds hollow, even to me. "My mum was." I think back to the beginning, to breaking into Mrs Marshall's that first time to look for the locket.

"How about a top-up?"

I hand over my mug.

Who would enjoy crawling around on the bathroom floor, getting soap scum on their trousers? But I found it, the necklace.

"Your tea's getting cold, dear."

I sip my tea, wincing at the bitter taste before adding more milk.

I found something else too. The lipstick case. The photos. With everything that's happened, I'd forgotten all about them. Who was he? Mrs Marshall's husband? But why hide them? No, Mrs Marshall must have been using the photos to blackmail someone. But they were hardly salacious, just an everyday sight at any swimming pool or beach. Hardly enough to blackmail someone with. Unless it's what the photo represented. An affair perhaps?

I wonder if they're still there. No, the police will have taken them as evidence.

"Nora, dear, you seem to have drifted off."

I smile apologetically. "I was miles away."

She returns the smile. "Somewhere nice? Perhaps with a handsome gentleman?"

"No, I was just thinking."

"Anything I can help with, dear?" She tops up my tea.

"I just can't believe it's over. It feels…" It feels no different. They still have to prove the confession was written by Paul Marshall, maybe then… But why confess? The police weren't closing in. And even if they were, why make it easy for them? It doesn't make sense.

"Would you like some cake, dear?" Mrs Baillie stands

beside me, holding a large slice of cake.

"Thank you." I place the plate on the table, my eyes suddenly heavy. The last few days have taken more out of me than I thought.

"You're daydreaming again, dear."

I shake my head. "Sorry, I… I don't…"

"My George was bad for that too." She hands me a silver picture frame, it slips from my fingers, landing on the floor by my feet.

Staring up at me is the man whose pictures I found in Mrs Marshall's lipstick case.

CHAPTER TWENTY-TWO

I stretch forward to pick up the picture. My fingers graze the frame before I flop back into the chair, my head swimming.

"Are you all right, dear?"

"Yes… yes. Just light-headed."

Mrs Baillie's knitting needles click. "That'll be the sedative, dear."

"The sed…"

"I didn't want to, dear. But you wouldn't stop, not until you knew the truth."

Pushing myself up, I try to stand. "The… truth?"

"About my killing Mrs Marshall."

"You…" My knees give way, dropping me onto the carpet.

"It was only a matter of time before you caught me. You nearly did. When I was hiding the drugs I used to kill Paul."

"Paul…"

"Yes, dear. That was me too, I'm afraid."

When Mum and I interrupted her gathering her wool. If we'd been any earlier…

I try to focus my eyes. "The pictures."

"Of my husband, yes dear. It wasn't an affair if that's what you're thinking. My George was a good, God-fearing man."

"He…"

"He was going senile towards the end. Mrs Marshall tricked him. She claimed to be his wife and he believed her. Well, why wouldn't he? I didn't even know about the pictures, not at first."

I hear shuffling steps.

"They were nothing."

"Perhaps not to you, dear. These days nudity is everywhere."

"You killed…"

"I didn't mean to, dear. Surely you can understand that. I'd taken the cake round to plead with her but she just laughed. She said such cruel things about my George. I'm afraid I lost my temper. The cake was in my hand before I realised what I was doing. By the time I did, well, I thought, perhaps the world would be a better place without her." She strokes my hair. "Where are they?"

I shake my head. "Why Paul?"

"He caught me searching his mother's house." She sighs. "I told him I missed my friend. But, of course, he knew better."

"The drugs…"

"It wasn't planned, dear. I'm not a murderer, not really."

The carpet is rough on my cheek. Get up, Nora. Get up. "How…"

"I told you, dear, my George was a vet. When he passed, I couldn't bring myself to get rid of his things. I was in the cupboard, getting the money and his bag was just sitting there. I didn't even know if they'd work. But then, they did for George. He asked me to help him, you see, at the end. And I did. Well, you would, wouldn't you? If you loved someone. And I do love him. Death doesn't change that."

She's right, it doesn't. But that doesn't mean I'm ready to join Colin, not yet.

I dig my fingers into the carpet, trying to push myself up. Mrs Baillie pushes me back down. "I am sorry, dear, but you know too much. It'll be quick. Painless too. At least, I think it is."

She moves my hair aside, my vision goes black.

***

"Get up, Nora. Come on, get up."

Grumbling, I try to lift an arm to wave Mum away. Why is she waking me anyway? Then I remember. Mrs Baillie, the bitter tea, the confession. I try to speak.

"I've got her." The voice is familiar, male.

Strong arms pull me to my feet. I'm dragged, my legs trailing.

"Where the hell is that ambulance?" Mum sounds worried.

Say something, Nora, let her know you're okay.

"Come on, Nora, walk it off." The dragging continues.

"It's not working." Mum's voice breaks.

There's a loud knock before the room fills with noise.

"It's about time." Mum's angry, but I don't think it's at me. I'm lowered to the floor. A light shines in my eyes.

"What's her name?"

"Nora."

"Can you hear me, Nora?"

Mumble.

"Okay, let's get her onto the stretcher." I'm lifted and everything fades again.

***

"How do you expect her to get better eating this tripe?"

Someone sighs. "I can assure you, Miss James, the meals here are well-balanced."

There's a scuffle.

"Need I remind you that they're for your daughter?"

"I'm just testing it to make sure you lot aren't trying to poison her. Tastes like you are."

"Why would we purposely poison people?"

A tut. "To cut down on the demands on the NHS, obviously."

Another sigh. "Call me if she needs anything."

"She needs another cuppa. With sugar this time."

I open my eyes as the nurse retreats, cup in hand. I'm surprised she didn't hit Mum with it. Maybe she's waiting until it's full.

"Nora?"

I smile. At least, I think I do. I'm still a little woozy.

"It's about time you woke up." She sniffs. "I had to miss strip spades."

My chest hurts when I laugh.

"Stop that. Just you rest." She pats my hand. "I've got my book here anyway."

Please don't be for Smutty Book Club.

She holds it up for me to see. Yep, that's for Smutty Book Club.

I shake my head. "How…"

"Well, I haven't got that far yet. He's an ex-navy SEAL who likes it rough, you know, Fifty Shades rough—"

I shake my head again, this time I know I'm smiling. "How did you find me?"

"I'm your Mum. Of course I found you."

I frown. What isn't she telling me? Mum shuffles under my gaze.

"How?"

"Through the tracker in my car."

The… "Why do you have that?"

"I… Well, I can't always find it." She sniffs. "Those multi-storeys are confusing. It all looks the same."

True, if you ignore all the signs telling you which level you're on.

I chuckle, it hurts less this time. Maybe that nurse gave me something nice to ease the heaviness.

"There was a man."

"An accomplice?" Mum sounds excited.

I frown. An accomplice? Then my mind clears. "No, with you."

"Oh, that was Matty. He gave me a lift to get— To rescue you."

"How did you know I was in trouble?"

"That was the car too. You knew I needed it back so when you didn't show, I knew something was up. At first, I hoped you'd just got luc— Your date had gone well. But when the tracker showed you were at Calburn Court, I knew something must have happened."

To her car, something must have happened to her car.

"So Matty drove me over, and Barbie said you'd gone to see Sammy, but then Sammy said you'd left. After that, I figured there was only one other place you could be."

I consider this. "You went for cake, didn't you?"

Mum's cheeks flush. "Nora! How could you say such a thing?"

Yep, cake.

"Anyway, that's when we found you."

After she barged in in her usual manner, no doubt.

"Thankfully, it was only a small dose. The doctor — who's about twelve if he's a day — says you'll be fine and can come home soon."

Home. That sounds nice. Mrs Baillie seemed nice, too. "What'll happen to her?"

"Mrs Baillie? I'm not sure. There may not be any barnacles on her brain, but she's as crazy as a hairy haggis hunter."

"Who's hairy, the haggis or the hunter?" Did I just say that? I must be worse than I thought. "She made good cakes though."

Mum sniffs. "Matty wouldn't let me take that one from the kitchen, said it might have been poisoned. Bet it'd have tasted amazing either way."

My mum, the only person who can get upset about not being allowed to eat potentially poisonous produce. It's amazing she's lasted this long.

"Thank Mr Pender for me."

"You can thank me yourself. I accept payment in the form of kisses on the cheek and cold hard cash." Mr Pender grins at me from behind an enormous bouquet of roses. For a minute, I'm tempted to ask if he picked them from Mrs Baillie's garden. But, of course, he didn't.

I inhale their beautiful scent. Am I imagining the hint of dog poo?

"Thank you, Mr Pender. For everything."

"It's Matty, Nora. And it's not me you need to thank. Your mum's the real hero. I just called for backup, more to rescue Mrs Baillie than anything else."

I frown. "You didn't stop Mrs Baillie?"

He laughs. "Are you kidding? Your mum had her in a chokehold before I even knew something was wrong."

Mum blushes. "You'd have done the same for me."

I smile. She's right, I would.

***

DI Buchanan interviews me that night, with much protesting from Mum. At one point, I thought he was going to have her escorted from the building. But, as usual, she manages to talk her way out of it. Now, if she could just stop talking herself into trouble in the first place…

More surprising is the visit from Barbara Veitch. While I was being slowly drugged by the murderous Mrs Baillie, Barbara was discovering the *real* meaning behind Paul Marshall's note. He'd helped himself to money from her safe to pay off the loan sharks. The police found the money in his mother's bedroom, under all those clothes. They didn't know where it had come from until Barbara called them. By the time they arrived, I was being wheeled towards the ambulance.

Barbara almost seemed apologetic about the mix-up. Almost.

I'm discharged from hospital the following morning, or as Mum calls it, transferred into her custody for an extended period of rehab. I think she overheard one of the Physiotherapists saying that last bit.

The nurses look pleased to see the back of Mum as we pack my belongings and head for the exit. I even think I hear a cheer as the ward door closes behind us.

Mum insists on carrying my bags, which, of course, involves pointing her assets at a porter and having him carry the cases.

Car packed, we head for home and a decent cup of tea. Mum's less than amused when I suggest we swing by a local coffee shop to get one.

Debbie Hall is walking up our garden path as we pull into the driveway. She waves a greeting. "I was just dropping off a get-well card, but I see they've let you escape."

"Come in for tea." Mum unlocks the front door.

"I'd love a cup if you're sure you're up to having visitors." She looks at me, uncertainly.

I want to warn her not to drink Mum's tea, but Mum's ushering her towards the kitchen before I get the chance. Poor woman.

"I'm glad I caught you. I wanted to talk about your job." Debbie moves aside some newspapers and sits at the table. "After the story hit the Moorbank Gazette, I was inundated with people telling me that Mrs Marshall had pulled a similar trick with them, making false accusations and then blackmailing them."

Mum places a greasy-looking cup of tea in front of Debbie.

Don't drink it, Debbie, not unless you need a laxative.

"The article mentioned that you'd worked for Hall-In, and at first, I thought that was it. But I've had phone call after phone call demanding your reinstatement." She eyes the tea before taking a large gulp. She's braver than me.

The doorbell rings and Mum excuses herself. Debbie continues. "Your job's still there if want it."

I grin. "When can I start?"

"How about next Monday? Give you a chance to recover."

"Thanks, Debbie."

Debbie holds up her mug and we clink them together. "Welcome back, Nora." She takes another gulp of tea. "I tell you one thing, it's certainly not dull having you around."

Mum returns, beaming. "Nora, you've got a visitor." She steps aside. I swear I feel my jaw drop as I stand to greet our guest.

"Hello. You must be Mrs McGinty's third cousin."

The End

GLOSSARY:

The Murder in Moorbank series is set in various fictitious towns in West Lothian, Scotland, and is written in UK English. Throughout Chocolate Cake and a Corpse, some terms are used that you may or may not be familiar with. If you're not, I hope you find these brief definitions useful.

Thanks for reading,

Susi J. Smith

Glossary of Terms

BAIRN: Child.

THE BARRAS: The Barras is a well-known market in Glasgow.

BLETHER: To talk a lot, or to have a chat. E.g. 'she's such a blether' (she talks a lot); 'Och, I was just having a blether' (I was just having a chat).

BOOT: What Americans call the trunk of a car.

CRABBIT: Grumpy. A 'crabbit Annie' is just a colloquial term for a grumpy woman.

DAB HAND: to be good at something. E.g. She's a dab hand at painting.

FIVER: Five pounds (Sterling).

GGS: Racehorses, or horse racing.

GLOOP: A thick liquid. Shampoo, for example.

HAGGIS: Surely everyone knows about the wild haggises that roam the Scottish glens, munching on heather (are you okay with 'munching'? If not, please replace it with 'eating', and remove the 'on'). All right, so they're not really wee creatures that taste nice with tatties (potatoes). It's a traditional dish made from the liver, heart, and lungs of a sheep. It tastes better than it sounds.

HALFERS: To go 50/50 on the cost of something.

HAVER/HAVERING: To talk nonsense/talking nonsense.

HOWK/HOWKING: A Scottish word that the online dictionary is convinced means 'to dig about'. In common usage here in West Lothian, it means 'to pull/pulling'. E.g. howk up your skirt.

LASS: Girl.

LAVVY: Toilet

LINO: Short for linoleum

NAFF: Unstylish, or unsophisticated. Not to be confused with 'naff off' which means 'go away'.

OCH: A guttural noise used to express emotions such as surprise, and disbelief.

PDSA: The People's Dispensary for Sick Animals (PDSA) is a charity which raises money to help animals.

POKE: This word has two different meanings. It can mean 'to prod', or it can mean a 'packet'. E.g. a poke of chips.

QUID: One pound (Sterling)

SHERIFF OFFICERS: the Scottish equivalent of bailiffs; legal debt enforcers.

SKINT: To have no money.

SOZZLED: Very drunk.

TELLY: Television

TENNER: Ten pounds (Sterling)

TRIPE: Technically, it is the edible stomach lining of an animal. However, in Chocolate Cake and a Corpse, it's used in the context of its second meaning: rubbish, nonsense.

WEE: Little

ABOUT THE AUTHOR

Susi J Smith lives in West Lothian, Scotland, where she longs for a writing room of her own. She is a member of a local writing group, West Lothian Writers.
For more information, check out her website:
https://susijsmith.wixsite.com/susi-j-smith or Facebook page: https://www.facebook.com/SusiJSmith/

Printed in Great Britain
by Amazon